"THIS IS TOO FAST!" SHE WHISPERED.

He sat back, his hands cradling her face. "It isn't in me to throw the race, Lindsay. And I've never wanted to win one more."

Lindsay pulled back from his touch. "How can you talk like that! You sound as if we've known each other for months instead of days!"

"There was something between us the second you walked in the door—we both know that," he said. "Other people's relationships may start out at a walking pace, but we were in a dead heat from the beginning. And you know it, even if you don't want to admit it."

"I don't believe any such nonsense. Not a word," she lied.

A CANDLELIGHT ECSTASY ROMANCE ®

WORKING IT OUT

Julia Howard

A CANDLELIGHT ECSTASY ROMANCE ®

Published by
Dell Publishing Co., Inc.
1 Dag Hammarskjold Plaza
New York, New York 10017

ISBN: 0–440–19789–9

Printed in the United States of America

First printing—June 1984

To Diane and Nancy,
and to
WRM III,
of course.

To Our Readers:

We have been delighted with your enthusiastic response to Candlelight Ecstasy Romances®, and we thank you for the interest you have shown in this exciting series.

In the upcoming months we will continue to present the distinctive sensuous love stories you have come to expect only from Ecstasy. We look forward to bringing you many more books from your favorite authors and also the very finest work from new authors of contemporary romantic fiction.

As always, we are striving to present the unique, absorbing love stories that you enjoy most—books that are more than ordinary romance.

Your suggestions and comments are always welcome. Please write to us at the address below.

Sincerely,

The Editors
Candlelight Romances
1 Dag Hammarskjold Plaza
New York, New York 10017

CHAPTER ONE

Lindsay Trent was lost in the abstract world of her computer program. The quiet of her new office in Pacific Beach helped her concentration, and she was close to discovering the bug in her code that had eluded her for days. She idly drew circles around the sprocket holes on the edge of the green-and-white-striped computer paper while her mind followed the trail of the program logic on the printout. That jump instruction referred back to—

Crash! She jumped in her seat and her pencil went flying.

"What's going on down there?" she cried to the room, empty except for herself and a half dozen computers placed on whatever flat surface was available. The noise came from the store below her office, a bike shop the real estate agent had assured her would never be noisy enough to bother her. She'd met Roger, the kid who ran the place, but she'd been here almost two weeks and he'd never disturbed her like this before.

Crash!

"Damn!" Flipping her long, dark braid over the back of the chair, she sat back with a scowl hovering around her blue eyes. She'd lost her train of thought and now she'd have to start back at the beginning *again*.

Sighing in disgust, she dug another pencil out of her desk drawer and turned the fan folds of the printout to the front, following her program from the beginning once more. This time, however, she didn't get past the first page before the crashing and banging started up again.

"What the hell is he doing?" she yelled. She stood up suddenly, sending her chair wheeling off the acrylic floor mat onto the beige carpet. She hesitated for a moment, but another crash sent her stomping to the door. Roger was going to discover he could *not* blithely act like Attila the Hun and get away with it!

She slammed outside and ran down the rustic stairs made from railroad ties that led from the second floor of the small, two-story office building to the sidewalk. In her anger she didn't feel the warmth of the early May sunshine or notice the cool breeze from the nearby Pacific that pulled at her T-shirt.

"Roger!" she said, walking through the open door of the Champion Bicycle Shop. But instead of looking behind the counter, her eyes automatically traveled to the poster on the opposite wall. She rarely noticed the brand of handmade bicycle frame it advertised but only saw the man who dominated it. He had casually slung a fully equipped bicycle over his right shoulder, the action emphasizing every muscle in his slender frame. He was blond, tan, and had the most devastating smile she'd ever seen.

Her eyes were still on the poster while she said, "Roger, just what the hell are you doing down here?" Embarrassed by her silly habit of looking at the poster every time she entered the shop, she spoke

12

more impatiently than she'd intended. "It sounds as if barbarian hordes are attacking," she said, turning toward Roger behind the counter. "Can't you be—" *Oh, my God, it's him!*

The nice, safe, two-dimensional image of the man in the poster stared back at her from behind the bicycle shop counter in three very real dimensions. A look of impatience swept over his features, and the striking bone structure of his face intensified the emotion. He turned back to the open drawer and riffled through its contents before slamming it shut with a loud crash.

The noise jarred Lindsay from her shock. "Who are you? Does Roger know you're pillaging through his counter?"

"It's *my* counter and I don't recall needing Roger's permission to go through it," he said. "And you may have noticed that the sign outside says *Kit Hawthorne's* Champion Bicycle Shop, not Roger Bailey's."

"Yours? But this is Roger's shop!"

His eyes traveled over her as if to ask who she thought she was to challenge him in his own store. She saw his derision as he took in the baggy T-shirt she wore that had once belonged to her brother; her limp, faded jeans and old running shoes with the seams gaping where the threads had worn through.

He opened another drawer, and his disinterested eyes left her to study its contents. That disinterest stung.

"Roger's?" he said, peering under a handful of papers that had been jammed carelessly into the drawer. "Are you crazy? He's a nice kid, but he has the business savvy of a crustacean." He raised his head, his green eyes revealing his impatience. "Are

13

you here to get a bicycle? Looks like it'd do you some good."

Stung again, she answered inanely, "It's just these clothes." No one would ever say she was too thin, certainly, but she didn't deserve that remark. It wasn't her fault her figure was considered lush instead of model thin; she was slender enough for her above-average height. She resisted an impulse to tuck in her T-shirt to show him that more clearly.

"Besides, I didn't come down here to look at bicycles, I came down to complain about the noise. The landlord assured me Roger's—your—bicycle shop was quiet!"

"It will be quiet, just as soon as I get rid of that electronic abomination," he said, pointing with his thumb toward an open office door.

She still hadn't forgiven him his earlier remark and her gaze held more frost than San Diego saw in a decade of winters, but she couldn't resist glancing through the open doorway. A microcomputer was sitting on a desk, crammed between stacks of paper on one side and assorted bicycle parts on the other. It looked very familiar.

"What abomination? All I see is a CRT."

"That *is* the abomination," he said. "I've knocked over two bikes and emptied nearly all our drawers trying to find the manual to fix that thing." His eyes narrowed as he looked more closely at her. "So you're Rog's new computer freak."

"I'm not a freak and I'm not Rog's!" she said, her cheeks flushing. "But I do work with computers and maybe I could help you—if it'll get you to quiet down."

"I thought Rog said you wrote games," he said.

"*Computer* games. But I write all kinds of software," she said, "It's my job."

"You're a programmer?" he asked, starting to rummage through another drawer.

"Sort of." How was she to tell him she and her twin brother Logan *owned* Trent Computer Systems and that she was in charge of software development for their entire line of computers.

"Ah-ha! Found the damn thing," he said, smiling and waving the computer manual. "Listen, if that offer to help is still open, I'll take you up on it."

That smile . . .

"Sure," she heard herself answering without the slightest idea she'd been going to.

He bowed slightly and ushered her into his tiny office, pulling out the desk chair for her to sit on. To her dismay, he remained in the room and hovered over her to watch.

He was so close she could feel the warmth from his body along her upper back and shoulders and smell his pungent masculinity. She gazed blankly at the "TCS LT-1050" logo at the lower right hand part of the screen cabinet for a moment, unable to think what to do next. She was startled when he handed her the computer manual with *Trent Computer Systems* blazoned across the top.

"When did you get this?" she asked. Her mind was still in the grip of the partial paralysis caused by his nearness, and she added without thinking, "It's our newest model."

"*Our?* Who are you?" he demanded.

"Lindsay Trent," she answered, grabbing a nearby box of diskettes to cover her sudden nervousness.

"*That* Trent?" he asked, pointing to the computer manual.

She nodded and tried to swallow, but her throat had become too dry and her tongue only stuck to the roof of her mouth. Forcing herself to move, she turned the system on and put a diskette into the upper slot of the disk drive next to the screen.

"Well, if anybody can fix this thing, I guess you should be able to," he said, leaning forward still farther. She could feel his hip press into her shoulder and she had to struggle to keep her reaction to his blazing hot touch from showing.

She pushed the small red switch on the side of the computer to "boot" the operating system program into the computer's memory. A row of *at* signs appeared at the top of the screen, a sure indication someone at the store where he'd bought the machine hadn't flipped the right internal switches.

She started to stand so she could reach the tiny rocker switches at the back of the machine, but Kit's hand fell on her shoulder and kept her from rising. "How quickly can you get it fixed? I've been hassling with it ever since I got back from Santa Barbara and I couldn't get it to do a thing."

"I'm not quite done," she said, standing. Her actions forced him to drop his hand, but he was perilously close to crowding next to her to see what she was doing. She froze for a brief moment, but the sound of several people entering the store and calling for Kit drew him out of the office.

She inhaled deeply and exhaled in a long, drawn-out sigh, not sure if the sigh was of relief or regret.

Hearing but not understanding the technical cycling talk from the outer room, Lindsay quickly found a battered screwdriver and a sharp pencil. It took only a moment to unscrew the computer terminal's cover and flip a couple of tiny switches with the point of the pencil. She booted the system again and grinned when she was rewarded with an operating system message in English instead of gibberish.

Lindsay rose to go and tell Kit his computer was ready to use, but a burst of laughter from the bicyclists slowed her movements. Quietly standing in the small office doorway, she inhaled to explain she was done, but her natural breath turned into a silent gasp. Kit was placing a ten-speed on the working rack and tightening the clamp, his actions delineating the muscles in his shoulders and arms.

Her reaction was sudden and unexpected. A wave of heat broke over her as if she'd stepped into the path of a Santa Ana wind, threatening to disburse her well-ordered emotions as easily as the fluff of a dandelion.

A rhythmic thumping came to her ears, and she felt a moment of consternation. Surely her heart wasn't beating that loudly! Then she recognized the increasingly familiar sound of a skateboard on the sidewalk and laughed to herself, taking a deep breath to steady her shaky pulse.

Through the front window she could see Roger doing a loop on the back wheels of his skateboard. He ended by kicking the skateboard into the air, catching it under his arm and calmly sauntering into the bike shop.

"Hey, Kit, how was Santa Barbara? Heard your numbers for the time trial were fa-a-a-n-n-n-tastic." Dark brown hair escaped the headband he wore, letting the heavily sun-streaked curls dance on his neck as he nodded to the others in the room. Roger grinned when he noticed Lindsay standing in the doorway to Kit's office.

"Hey, Lin, how's it goin'?" he asked. The sparkle

17

in his brown eyes didn't dim a bit when he added in a loud aside to Kit, "So you met the computer lady, huh? I've been trying to convince her I'm as 'user friendly' as her machines up there, but no luck." His woebegone expression was hampered by the grin still tugging at the corners of his mouth.

Kit laughed. "User friendly? After all that talk about dragons and deadly trolls? Not to mention getting killed off three times in less than an hour." Lindsay smiled at the sally, bringing out the dimple in her right cheek. Kit's green eyes darkened as they watched her, adding, "That's not my idea of friendly."

Her smile became self-conscious under that intent gaze and finally disappeared. "Roger was playing my computer game, Timecast. It can be pretty tricky."

"I don't know about dragons," Kit said dryly, "but my ledger program's probably going to put up a tough fight."

Lindsay stood silent for a moment. It was amazing how his eyes seemed to tilt up at the ends just before he was going to smile. Her knees felt wobbly, like they had the first time she'd gone roller skating.

"Your computer's all set," she said quickly and started walking toward the door to escape. "The baud rate wasn't set right." She was almost on the threshold when a sudden impulse made her add, "Let me know if you have any trouble with your ledger program. I'll try to see what I can do."

How she managed to wave good-bye to Roger and calmly walk out of the bike shop, she didn't know. But as soon as her foot touched the first step, she bounded up the stairs to her office, not at all sure why it felt as if she were skirting the edge of an unseen abyss.

Once inside the door, Lindsay rubbed the bridge of her nose in agitation. Her reaction to discovering Kit Hawthorne had caught her by surprise, but now she dismissed her uneasy feeling with a sigh and a wave of her hand. Carefully keeping her mind blanked, she righted the chair that had fallen over when she'd rushed from the room and sat down, leaning back with her feet on the desk.

It wasn't working. She couldn't stop thinking of him. The coded instructions on the printout in her lap kept blurring into images of Kit when he'd lifted the bike onto the repair rack, and her mind's eye kept following the tantalizing flow of his muscles. Where was all her famous discipline? And where had all her training gone? M.A. degrees in computer software engineering didn't dissipate in the sun like a weatherman's early morning cloudiness.

She shook her head ruefully while snapping at the perforated folds of the computer paper with her thumb and index finger. True, few people could immerse themselves in a subject the way Lindsay Trent could. A one-track mind was fine, except when that one track insisted on leading her to Kit Hawthorne instead of the Z80 assembly program resting in her lap.

It all came back to that damn poster—or rather the man in it. To Lindsay, the slender but muscular man it pictured had been exotic, like mysterious spices from the Orient, and she'd idly concocted innocent fantasies about him. Well, some were not so innocent, she amended, feeling the heat of a blush spread up her neck. But it was unnerving to have a nice safe picture suddenly appear in the flesh. And in *what* flesh.

Lindsay felt her cheeks grow hot with another blush. "It's damned unnerving," she repeated aloud, taking her feet off the desk and leaning forward. She threw her printout—now in two pieces—onto the desk. "So watch it. And keep a tight rein on your imagination. God knows what else might show up."

A deep chuckle froze her to her chair. But in the next moment she spun around to see Kit leaning nonchalantly in the doorway, his arms crossed in front of him and his shoulder against the doorjamb. In a panic-stricken replay, she reviewed what she'd just said, and though it was hard to differentiate between what she'd said aloud and what she'd said silently, Lindsay didn't think she had let anything incriminating escape.

He smiled. "That look! But I suppose I deserve it. I wasn't exactly polite to you."

"No, no, I was just startled, that's all," she said. "I wasn't expecting anyone. It's too early for my brother and his friends." *Babble, babble.* "Would you like something to drink? I've got some diet soda."

"No kidding," he said, his smile widening. His eyes followed the stacks of empty diet soda cans lining one wall as he entered her office. She rose and started toward the tiny kitchenette in the far corner of the room until his hand forestalled her.

"But I'll take a rain check on the drink," he said. "I really came up here to thank you and apologize for being such a bear when you first walked into my shop."

Lindsay shook her head to tell him an apology wasn't necessary; the way she'd barged into his shop hadn't left much room for politeness. And "bear" was the last word she'd use for the slender man hitching one muscle-sculptured thigh onto the edge of a computer table. His grace reminded her not of the predatory sinuousness of a panther but of the awesome power of a leashed puma—leashed, but not tamed.

She had never been this near someone who was so overwhelmingly physical. She nervously tucked her hands into the back pockets of her cutoffs, pulling the T-shirt taut across her ample breasts and slim waist and causing a look of appreciation—and specu-lation—to flash into his malachite eyes.

"Ah, is your ten-fifty still working okay?" she asked brightly, trying to hide a sudden need to sit down. Grabbing the closest chair, she sat in the chair in front of the computer table Kit was sitting on, adding, "This is the same model, though Logan—my brother—has modified it a bit. Let me show you some of the things it can do." Her fingers positioned themselves over the keyboard, but he reached over to stop her.

"I'd rather see some of the things you can do, Lindsay," he said, his voice low as he caressed her hand.

"Wha—what do you mean?" Half a minute passed before she remembered to snatch her hand away from his touch.

"Why, what kind of work you do here, of course. What else could I possibly mean?" His devastating smile lit his lips again, and Lindsay had to grab for a disk to cover her reaction.

My God! This guy's way *out of my league!* Lindsay popped a disk into drive A and booted the system. *Oh, for the simple, placid—and definitely nonphysical —computer nerds at Trent Computer Systems!*

"Basically—if you'll pardon the pun—I develop

21

software for Trent Computer System's computers. We've got five different models, each one geared to a different market," she said, sliding her chair farther from him and indicating the other computers in her office. "Real estate, travel agencies, yours is for general office use, and a couple are geared to the home computer market. Personal computers, you know."

"May I look?" he asked, indicating the box of disks she still held in her lap. "What about the game Rog played? Is it in here?"

"I think Timecast is in there. . . ." she said. Lindsay stood and leaned over the box that was resting casually on his thigh.

The magnificent muscles on the tops of his thighs tapered to a point at his knees, and she struggled to keep her eyes from following the enticing lines under his jeans. He was very slender—the bottom of his rib cage was delineated under his T-shirt—but so well muscled that his male frame was highlighted rather than diminished by that slenderness.

To a woman who was used to the pale, soft, pudgy men so common in the computer field, Kit was intoxicatingly different . . . exotic. She shook her head and reached for one of the eight-inch disks. *How can you so easily forget what happened to Logan? You don't need that kind of pain, too.*

"Here it is," she said, ending the long, breathing silence. "It takes quite a while to play it when you first start, but I can show you if you'd like."

"I'll take a rain check then, if only because it's a good excuse to let me come back," he said, handing the disk box back to her. She could feel his gaze warming her, though a pinprick of anxiety went through her when his eyes tightened at the edges as if he was suddenly assessing her in a new light. "Now let me get this right. You *own* Trent Computer Systems, right?"

"Half. My brother Logan owns the other half. But he does a lot of the traveling—setting up new systems, trouble-shooting, and so forth."

He tilted his head to one side, and his eyes narrowed further. After quickly scanning the room, his eyes came back to her. "Public stock?"

"No, it's privately held." She unconsciously brushed back the wisps of dark hair that inevitably escaped from her braid, while a tiny frown pulled at the corners of her mouth. "Why the third degree, inspector?" she asked, hoping to let him know gently that his questions were close to trespassing on confidential matters.

He smiled his apology, and her frown lost its strength. "Sorry. I was just curious as to why someone who's at the top of a successful company like Trent goes around in ancient running shoes and a T-shirt obviously sized for a Charger linebacker instead of a Charger fan and drives that Mustang convertible I saw in your space in the parking lot. Where's the Ferrari?"

That smile was much too potent, and Lindsay backed away and sat down at her desk, a good safe five feet away. She plucked at the baggy gold and blue cotton and laughed. "I haven't had *time* to change my life-style! High tech is hot, but it's also as competitive as hell. TCS has to have the best there is to stay on top, and half that job is mine." She shrugged, adding, "But I've never been into the whole nouveau riche thing anyway. Logan and I are in this field because we like it, not because we have an insatiable desire for Rolex watches and Louis

Vuitton luggage." She smiled again. "Not to mention Ferraris."

Kit moved from the computer table to the chair she'd been sitting in before and rolled it to the edge of the floor mat, closing the distance between them by a good two feet. She wasn't so safe anymore.

"But what about you?" she asked quickly. "According to Rog, you're a world-class cyclist, finishing high in the ranking at the Tour de France, Tour of Flanders, races in Italy I can't begin to pronounce, *and* you were on the two previous Olympic teams. Surely you've gotten at least a Corvette if not a Ferrari out of all that."

Kit laughed, a thoroughly masculine but a joyful and oddly melodic sound. "I'm afraid there's more glory than gold in cycling. And what I did get for promoting products and such I funneled back into my shops here for my retirement."

"But that's a long way off!"

Something close to a sigh escaped him and he straightened in his chair, causing a lock of his sun-color hair to fall onto his forehead. When he looked up, his green eyes had darkened to the shade of a forest in shadow.

"Four months, to be exact," he said. He bent slightly from the waist in a mock bow and added, "At the ripe old age of thirty-four, Christopher Hawthorne is leaving the ranks of the professional cyclist to rejoin the amateurs. Of course, once I turned pro I made myself ineligible for Olympic contention, but I can participate in other races that don't award prize money."

He grinned at her expression. "Don't look so sad! I had a good seventeen years in competition, and that reputation has helped me establish my bike shops."

His chair slid off the edge of the floor mat, making a slight thunk as he closed the remaining gap between them. He gently tucked a wisp of dark hair behind her ear and let his fingers trail down the soft hidden flesh he found there. "You see, we both have something in common, being in fields that our talents and passions have drawn us to."

Leaning back to break the spell he'd woven, he added lightly, "But to be in a field you love *and* have all that money sounds pretty good to me. Are you sure you don't have a secret cache of furs somewhere?"

Despite his nearness, Lindsay laughed. "No, I don't! If something does strike my fancy, it's nice to be able to buy it, but fortunately I don't often see things I want!" *Except now,* a hidden voice murmured as desire for Kit pulled at her like an undertow at the beach.

The emotion caught her unaware, and she couldn't prevent a blush from scarleting her cheeks. To cover her embarrassment and avoid the curious look in Kit's eyes, she started rummaging through the printouts and manuals on her desk. Discovering the corpse of yesterday's burrito, stiff and surrounded by the orange blood of congealed grease on the bier of its wrapper, she wrinkled her nose and dumped it into the trash can.

Kit didn't even try to hide his smile of amusement. "Why don't you use the kitchen over there to fix yourself something decent?" he asked.

"Oh, it's just easier to walk down the street to Del Taco or Carl's."

He stood and walked past her to the trash can. Picking it up, he stared down into it and shook his head. "Tell you what—I owe you one for fixing my computer, so tomorrow *I'll* fix you a midday feast. How's that sound?"

The burrito slid to the bottom of the can with a loud thunk when he set the can back down. He chuckled for a moment before a quick frown sharpened his features. "Wait, I forgot tomorrow's Saturday, and only shop owners have to work six days a week."

"Shop owners and computer programmers," she said without thinking.

But he didn't give her a chance to retract her impulsive confession. "You'll be here? Great! Is a little after noon okay?"

The curl he'd tucked behind her ear had escaped again. Kit grasped it lightly and let it run through his fingers like dark threads of precious silk.

She could only nod.

"Tomorrow, then," he said, his voice subdued as he headed for the door.

She sat staring at the open doorway. How could she have given in like that! Office building etiquette required only a nodding friendliness, not long chats and luncheon dates—with Kit acting as a personal chef, no less! The phone interrupted her musings and she was thankful when Logan's voice snapped her attention back to her programming.

After getting an update on her brother's latest project, Lindsay gathered the two pieces of the assembly-language program she'd been working on earlier and tucked them under her arm. She checked the security system and closed her office, thinking that Kit's friendliness was motivated by nothing more than that—friendliness—and that after this initial period of eager acquaintance, they'd fall into the routine of an occasional nod in passing.

The traffic in Pacific Beach at quitting time was horrendous, and she made her twelfth vow in as many days not to leave her office right at five o'clock. Unfortunately, she never did remember that vow until it was too late, so fifteen minutes later she was waiting in a long line at the light at Garnet Avenue and Mission Boulevard when several bicyclists passed her.

She supposed having the top down on her convertible made it easy for him to identify her, because when the last cyclist rode by, she saw it was Kit, turning to give her that heart-stopping smile of his and wave. Her eyes automatically followed him as he stopped at the light with the others, obviously intent on the signal.

To Lindsay's astonishment, he never took his feet off the pedals but held the front wheel at a slight angle to the rest of the bike and gently rocked the bike back and forth to remain upright. When the signal changed and he accelerated, the muscles in his legs were sharply delineated even at four car-length's distance, and Lindsay felt her own muscles contract slightly in response.

She had a sinking feeling that to remain just friends with Kit Hawthorne was going to be a difficult fight—with herself. And there was more at stake than Lindsay's heart.

CHAPTER TWO

With one leg tucked under her, Lindsay sat studying the program spread out on her dining room table. It was nearly midnight and she was no closer to finishing the step-through than she had been three hours ago. The knuckles of her left hand dug into her cheek as she watched the pencil in her right hand idly drawing around the circles she'd drawn earlier around the sprocket holes.

When had that been? A lifetime ago—before a poster had come alive in front of her eyes. Was this how Dorothy felt when she woke up in Oz? Bemused and scared, but filled with wonder and excitement, too.

Lindsay threw the pencil onto the table and watched it roll off onto the carpet.

"Stop being an idiot. We can't afford another fatal Trent attraction to a physical fitness freak."

The picture of Kit when he'd smiled at her as he'd ridden past her car flashed through her mind, but it was quickly replaced by a similar image of Logan's ex-wife.

Mara had been into jogging, not cycling, but the

moving image was the same. Logan had been completely infatuated with her, and Lindsay, with a twin's empathy, had felt all his initial confusion and then his searing pain as the realization hit him that Mara's jogging partners were doing more than running.

A stab of anger mixed with pain shot through Lindsay. When Mara had finally understood that the gravy train was about to end, she'd hired one of the state's finest divorce lawyers and suddenly begun an Oscar-winning performance as the poor misunderstood wife of a slightly unbalanced computer genius. How could she have maligned Logan like that! Those courtroom scenes still hurt. And still Logan never quite grasped that his blond, ethereal Mara wasn't the woman he'd thought she was.

He may not have understood, but Lindsay had. Though she'd never forgive the woman who had almost destroyed her brother—not to mention Trent Computer Systems—with her rapacious requests, she had to acknowledge that the relationship had been a foregone disaster. They had been too different.

Logan had understood *nothing* of the world that Mara lived in, a world largely of the senses and emotions. It was certainly not a world a logical, scientific mind like his could even begin to comprehend. And Mara hadn't even tried to get a glimmer of Logan's world—except for the part that issued the checks.

They had been too different. Just as she and Kit were too different. And if Lindsay remembered nothing else of Logan's trauma, she remembered the bone-chilling terror she had felt when Mara's lawyer had announced that the wronged wife deserved controlling stock in the company to soothe her wounded sensibilities. On that day she'd vowed from the depths of her soul to never, *never* allow the company that was so much a part of her to be jeopardized again.

Lindsay's eyes focused on the green bars of the computer paper, and for a moment the cryptic instructions of the assembly-language program appeared as alien as the runes on a Celtic stone monument. Now TCS was almost completely free of Mara and her courtroom histrionics, and the company certainly didn't need another disaster to follow on the heels of the last one.

But Kit was totally unlike anyone she'd ever known, so completely different that even the specter of Mara couldn't diminish the ache her body had felt when he'd been so close to her that afternoon. She felt lost again in an Oz-like world where the rules she thought she knew and lived by were suddenly superfluous. If only she could tightly close her eyes and click her heels together to return to her Kansas—the safe, insular world of her computers.

It was a typical spring day in San Diego—overcast, with the promise of a glorious day later in the morning—though Lindsay didn't notice. She carefully put the top back up on her Mustang and headed for the stairs to her office.

Tired and groggy from lack of sleep, the last thing she wanted to do was walk past the windows of Kit's bike shop, but it was either that or walk all the way around the building. Ignoring the noises of the Saturday beach crowd, she trudged along the sidewalk and started up the old railroad tie steps.

Her mind was unruly that morning, and she grimly wondered if the women she'd seen in Kit's shop yesterday had knees that creaked as they walked up a stairway or if they breathed hard when they reached the top. She doubted it.

"Lindsay! Good morning," Kit called from the bottom step, looking disgustingly awake. "It's going to be a beautiful day, isn't it?"

She started to reply, but her optic nerves finally woke her reluctant brain and, with her normal defenses still down, Lindsay felt the full impact of Kit Hawthorne in places that had been quiescent for much too long. *There ought to be laws against looking like that.*

His clothes gave new meaning to the word "snug"; in fact, "poured into" wouldn't be too far off. The black Lycra "skin shorts" came down to a few inches above his knees, though neither the shorts nor the short-sleeved jersey he wore hid anything other than his tan.

The lack of sun made his eyes dark and unreadable, though they seemed to widen as they took in her white V-neck cotton knit top and blue shorts. When she didn't answer, he walked up a couple of steps and leaned against the railing. "You okay? I just wanted to remind you about lunch. Noon, remember?"

When he moved his muscles flowed beneath the shiny black surface, and Lindsay had to blink and shake her head to clear it. *How can I possibly be reacting like this?*

"Noon's fine, Kit," she managed to get out through a throat tight from her effort to control any visible reactions. "You don't have to do this, you know." *Maybe I'm having a remission of adolescence —complete with raging hormones.* She shook her head again. *At twenty-eight?*

"I know, but I want to, Lindsay," he said, giving

31

her a brief wave as he descended to the sidewalk. "I want to."

Lindsay ran the magnetically encoded plastic card through the security-system slot and entered her office. She threw the pages of her program onto the desk. "That's *not* how to step-through a program, Lin my girl!" The edges were completely doodled over, and she must have filled in every "o," "p" and "d" in the entire thing.

Firing up the ten-fifty near her desk to reprint the program, she reached for the chair and stopped. It was still half off the floor mat, just as Kit had left it the afternoon before, and her brief attempt to ignore her reactions on the steps was shattered.

The sudden, familiar clatter of the printer helped her recover from the almost debilitating realization that *now,* at last, she knew how Logan could have jeopardized everything. Physical movement helped to ease away the shock of that discovery, and she kneeled to pick up a pencil that had rolled under the desk.

She could feel rather than hear the creaking of her knees, and a mocking smile turned up the corners of her mouth. *She,* however, was fortunate that she could never compete with those Amazons she'd seen in Kit's shop yesterday.

Her mirror that morning had left no doubt that she would never be able to come close to their boyishly thin figures and narrow profiles—not when her slim waist blossomed upward into full breasts and downward into hips that, while they were in proportion to the rest of her, could never be taken for anything but female.

Somehow she got through the morning, though she only remembered half of what she did. But as it

32

neared twelve she couldn't hide her disgust with herself every time her eyes would stray to the clock on the wall over the sink.

It was like a bad closed loop in one of her programs. Her eyes would go to the clock . . . she'd catch herself doing it and lower her eyes . . . her gaze would fall to the sink, which would remind her of the promised lunch . . . which would make her avert her eyes . . . upward to the clock.

Just as she managed to cajole her attention back to her program, quick, exuberant steps on the stairs outside announced someone coming to her office. *Steady, girl.* She tried to remember the cool nerves that used to get her through a three-hour test on differential equations back in school, but as the steps rapidly neared, her cool nerves were no match for the blood pounding in her veins, warm with anticipation.

"Hey, what's happenin'," Rog said as he crossed the threshold. He stopped two steps into the room. "Why the dark?"

"Hi. Oh, I just never opened the blinds," she said unsteadily. She was feeling let down, but she didn't want to acknowledge the strength of it. To cover her reaction she went and yanked hard on the plastic chains on every thin-slated blind in the room, sending them folding up to the ceiling with a loud bang.

The noise and action helped her nerves somewhat, and Lindsay turned back to Roger with a satisfied smile. His brown eyes were wide with anxiety—her reaction was clearly something he didn't know how to deal with.

Looking at the four blindless windows, he swallowed convulsively. "I, uh, I, uh, Kit just asked me to tell you he'll be here in a few minutes. He had to go pick something up at the store."

33

When Kit walked through the door twenty minutes later, Lindsay felt a pang of regret that he'd changed from his skin shorts and jersey into a pair of jeans, soft and pale with age, and a T-shirt advertising an Italian brand of something she didn't recognize.

"Beautiful," he said, letting his eyes run over her enticing form. He carried an ice chest and a sack of groceries to the kitchenette, apologizing for being late. "My friend Jenny came in at the last minute needing a couple of new spokes, so I couldn't get to the store on time." He started lining up the contents of the grocery bag on the cutting board over the sink: vegetables, vegetables and more vegetables.

"I could have gone to the store for you," she said, restraining herself from peeking into the bag to find the hot dogs or hamburgers.

"Thanks, but there's this great place to get really fresh produce just over in Clairemont. It's hell to find, though." He briefly rinsed a couple of cherry tomatoes and popped them into his mouth while continuing to rinse some of the other things he'd bought.

"Isn't there anything I can do?" she asked, watching with awe as he started to slice and chop expertly. "Would you like a diet soda?"

He smiled. "The dinner tab includes drinks. There's some apple juice in the ice chest." He popped another tomato into his mouth. "Hope you've got some glasses."

Lindsay just stared at him for a moment. He was munching on *tomatoes!* Nobody munched on tomatoes. Potato chips, corn chips, cheese puffs, maybe peanuts . . . but tomatoes?

"Is something wrong?" Kit asked, pausing in his

34

chopping for a moment. "Don't you have any glasses?"

"Glasses? No, no, I don't." Was that really bean curd he was getting out of the ice chest? "What are we having for lunch? It looks—interesting; certainly not what I expected," she said, hoping he didn't catch the note of doubt in her voice. If this was the kind of stuff he normally ate, no wonder he was so slender.

"This is just a stir-fry dish. I didn't think you'd want anything too heavy on a day like today," he said, finishing up the vegetables. He pulled a large skillet out of the grocery bag and set it on one of the tiny stove's two burners, turning the heat up high. "Next time we can have a real meal—I make one fine mushroom pâté."

"Kit," Lindsay began, "do you eat, that is, are you a—"

"Vegetarian?" Kit finished for her. "Uh-huh. Does that bother you?"

She was leaning back against her desk, her arms folded under her breasts. A tiny crease formed between her eyes. "No, it doesn't *bother* me, but I am surprised. I mean you don't seem like—" She broke off again, realizing she was suffering from acute foot-in-mouth disease.

"What you're trying to say without saying it is that I don't look like the people who go around chanting mantras with sheets wrapped around them." When she sighed and nodded, he smiled. "You don't have to worry. I won't start hitting you up for spare change."

That smile took away her strength and gave her courage at the same time. "Well, if it's not for religious reasons, why *are* you a vegetarian?"

35

"I do eat fish, if that helps your opinion of me." He dropped a piece of onion into the skillet and watched it sizzle.

He positioned two plates near the edge of the counter and then quickly started tossing the piles of vegetables he'd cut up into the hot skillet. Onions first, then water chestnuts and cashews; he added the mushrooms and tomatoes last.

Over the hiss from the skillet he said, "There're a thousand theories on the diet that lets a person's body metabolize food optimally. I tried a lot of them, but a vegetarian diet made me feel the best I ever had, and my performance really improved, too. That was six years ago, and I'm still alive and healthy."

"Alive" and "healthy" were definitely two words she would use to describe Kit Hawthorne. "I can see that," she managed to say without letting the incredible understatement show in her tone. But his diet only added another brick to the wall of differences between them, and Lindsay was subdued when he handed her a plate piled high with the strange-looking meal.

Absently taking a bite as she walked to the sofalike futon in the corner, she tried to think of ways to extricate herself from the budding relationship Kit seemed prepared to have. She was not going to let herself fall for a male version of Mara—but it was difficult right then to think of pain when her taste buds were having such a wonderful time.

"Hey, this is good! I love things that are crunchy."

"Glad you like it," he said, sitting down next to her on the futon. "Here's the apple juice. We'll have to drink it cyclist-style—right out of the bottle."

She took the wide-mouth bottle he held out to her and put it to her lips, trying not to giggle. It tasted sweet and crisp, just as her imagination had thought Kit would taste. . . . She choked slightly and handed the bottle back to him. Where had *that* thought come from?

But by the time the delicious meal was over and the kitchen had been cleaned up, the reserve Lindsay habitually assumed had disappeared and the bright, inquisitive and charming side of her personality began to shine through without her knowing it.

Kit sat close to her, and she leaned back into the corner of the futon, unconsciously trying to keep a barrier between them—even if the barrier was only of distance—but she couldn't deny the heady experience of having those verdant eyes gazing at her so intently. That attention made the afternoon fly quickly, and the day neared dusk without her noticing it.

"I know zip about cycling," she told him with a smile, watching the last rays of the sun make the golden depths of his hair look almost rococo in its splendor. "Rog tried to enlighten me, but I didn't understand most of it. He did seem impressed with your winning all those European races, though."

"I didn't win them, you know," he said softly and a bit absently, as if thinking of something other than what he was talking about. "Just placed fairly high in the rankings. The Europeans have been taking cycling seriously for a lot longer than Americans, and we've got a lot of catching up to do for those long road races of theirs."

Wisps of dark curls framed her face, having once again escaped the severity of her waist-length braid. Kit reached out and drew a finger along her hairline, making her forget what she had wanted to ask him.

Some vague question about American races danced out of reach when he spoke again.

"Do you always braid your hair?" he asked, leaning forward in the twilight of the room. His hand played with the tiny, sensitive hairs under her braid at the nape of her neck. "Why not something less severe?" He leaned closer, and she could feel his breath caressing her face, the barrier between them forgotten like a long-ago dream.

"It must be exquisite unbound. As exquisite as the rest of you . . ." he murmured, easing into a kiss.

She wasn't ready to be kissed. She wasn't ready for the shock of the sudden sensual storm that flashed and thundered through her. And she wasn't ready for her own acquiescence. She was returning his kiss.

Kissing and tasting—how could she have forgotten how good a man's mouth could taste? Had she ever known? But oh, how sweet and crisp he tasted, just as she'd imagined he would, and she savored it.

She ran her tongue along the inner line of his bottom lip and felt a shiver go through him that marked the end of his gentle exploration. His tongue thrust into her mouth, partnering hers in a dance of sensual fire.

Kit pulled her to him, and she yielded to the hard-pressing length of his body. She reacted on a sensuous level, her mind answering only with demands for the taste and touch her body suddenly required for sustenance.

She leaned into him, letting her hands slide under his shirt to discover by touch the dimple in the small of his back, the faint ridge of his ribs at his sides and the breadth of his shoulders. His skin was warm and smooth, and reveling in that warmth made her feel as if she were being enveloped in a comforter on a cold winter night.

Suddenly his hands stopped making slow, burning circles on her back and, gliding over her sides, caressed the swell of her breasts with a sensual deliberation that only made her ache for his touch.

Breathless, their lips parted, and she felt the yielding, glistening tip of his tongue tease the fine hairs in front of her ear. "Ah, my Lindsay, with eyes the color of a day in heaven, you're totally different from anyone I've ever met. Different and fascinating and such a glorious race to be won."

His words made her stiffen, but before she could react with anything beyond a gasped, "I'm not a race to be won!" there was a knock on her door.

"Lin, it's Logan," she heard her brother shout, followed by the half-muffled honk of a sneeze. At the first sound of his voice, Lindsay had jumped up to escape Kit's befuddling closeness, but her heart sank at the sound of the sneeze.

Only John Fenton sneezed quite like that—and if John was with Logan, her brother probably had the whole gang with him. She couldn't completely stifle her sigh of annoyance. The feelings Kit had called up from inside her were frightening—deliciously frightening—and she wanted to be alone to deal with them.

"Are you okay in there?" Logan called. But he didn't wait for her to answer and barged into the shadowed office. "Lin?" The room was suddenly noisy with six additional voices.

She stepped into the light provided by the last rays of the sun, and the other three young men and two women greeted her with casual friendliness. Kit remained near the futon, out of the light.

39

"Hi, Loge," she said. "I didn't expect to see you till tomorrow."

Logan shrugged and plopped down in a chair, smiling at her. His hair was the same deep brown, and had the look of a stylish cut that had gone untrimmed too long. His eyes were more gray than blue, and though his smile was genial, their usual good humor had been subdued for months now.

One of the men, tall and lanky, walked toward her desk. "How can you work in here?" he asked, squinting at the computer she'd been working on earlier. "Why don't you turn on a light? It's so dark."

Remembering Roger's similar comment, she glanced at the open blinds on the windows and a half-smile hovered around her lips. "I seem to be making a habit of it, Bob."

"It doesn't matter," Logan said, overriding whatever else she had been about to say. He paused a moment when John sneezed again, then said, "We came by to drag you off to that new grade-B sci-fi flick that's playing over in Mission Valley." Switching on the lamp on her desk, he added, "You've been working too hard anyway and you need a . . ." His voice trailed off as he caught sight of Kit standing near the futon.

Flushing at the sharp look her brother gave her, Lindsay stepped back out of the faint light coming through the windows into shadow. But she knew Logan didn't miss seeing the warmth in her cheeks— or Kit's handsome blond head and well-muscled frame. Watching his sister closely, Logan's eyes narrowed.

She took a deep, steadying breath. "This is Kit Hawthorne," she said, introducing him to the group in general. "He owns the bike shop downstairs." Kit gave her an enigmatic look that held a hint of challenge as he stepped next to her and shook Logan's hand.

"Kit, this is my brother Logan Trent, and these are some friends of ours: Bob Sperry," she said, indicating the lanky man still bent over the ten-fifty computer. She was desperately trying to keep her voice from shaking. *What was Logan thinking? Damn!* He'd never worn that inscrutable public mask until Mara had left, and now it was impossible to tell what was going on in his mind.

She quickly introduced the others: Heather McDonald, John Fenton, *sneeze*, Sue Knox, Monroe Harris. "They all work with us at Trent, in one form or another." And they were all good friends who right now she wished at Jericho.

"Listen, Kit," Logan said, "if you don't have other plans, why don't you join us?"

Lindsay glanced nervously at her brother. What was that odd note she detected in his voice? Not that it mattered; Kit was hardly the kind of man who went to low-budget movies.

"Thanks," Kit said. "Sounds like fun."

Standing next to him, she sucked in her breath in surprise. She'd seen the hard look that passed between her brother and Kit, and though she didn't know what it meant, she knew Logan had misjudged if he thought Kit could be put off by subtle intimidation. But *why* did Logan want to?

Kit put his hand on her waist to escort her out of her office. When she felt herself within his warm, firm grasp, she doubted if he could be put off by any kind of blatant intimidation. No one rose to the heights of as competitive a sport as cycling without knowing exactly how to win.

"Then let's go," Logan said. "It starts in half an hour."

At the last minute Lindsay remembered to release the blinds and turn on the security system. Kit waited for her to join him while the others trickled down the stairs.

"Since no one else has claimed you, I will," he murmured when she rejoined him. Feeling his hand on her waist again, she couldn't think of a good reason to tell him that the group of friends rarely paired up into couples. And when he added, the breath of his whisper intimately nipping at her ear, "You are a race, my Lindsay, and I plan on going the distance," she didn't want to think of anything at all.

The movie, a spectacular display of special effects and bad acting, left little impression on Lindsay. The jolts of red heat she felt came from Kit's arm fitting snugly across her shoulders, not the laser guns on the screen; and it wasn't the spaceships whizzing through the interstellar void that left her breathless but his fingers tracing the outline of her hand on the armrest between them.

Later, in the darkness of the theater parking lot, Lindsay could see her brother's eyes glint appraisingly at Kit. "I feel like some espresso," Logan said as they climbed into John's van. "Why don't we all go to the Blackbird in Marina Village?"

Fifteen minutes later they were crowded around one of the tiny wooden tables tucked into the corners of the charming coffee shop, drinking the rich, bitter espresso from small cups.

Logan set down his empty white china cup with a click and ordered another one. Lindsay was nervous, not sure which she should fear more: Kit's hard, heated body pressing into hers as they sat jammed

42

into the corner bench or her brother's disturbing, calculating coolness.

"So how's the bicycle business?" Logan asked Kit.

"Pretty good. San Diego's the perfect place for cycling," Kit answered politely, though she could feel the extra tension in him. "California's very fitness oriented, and that, plus our near-perfect weather, makes for a lot of people who like to ride."

"I suppose I have you to thank for all those kids on moto-cross bikes that swarm around TCS." The challenge in the words didn't match the challenge in the tone of Logan's voice. "That's why Lin and I had to move to different research facilities—it was too damn noisy."

"Yeah," Bob said, "remember that one kid who was always poppin' wheelies out by the delivery door? Damn near crashed into the UPS woman and destroyed a whole shipment of S-100 buses." He shook his head. "When I think of what *those* woulda cost to replace." He whistled to emphasize his point, and John, sitting on the outer side of Lindsay, sneezed in agreement.

She sighed in disgust. The noisy area where the building stood had little to do with why there'd been a major change in how TCS did business. They'd had to bring in a new outside chief executive officer to reorganize the entire company to save it from the devastations Mara's demands had caused. "C'mon, you guys, knock it off. Kit doesn't even sell those kinds of bikes. He sells ten-speed racing cycles—for people who take the sport seriously."

"Racing bikes, huh?" Logan said. "Do any racing yourself?"

"A little." The smile in Kit's eyes shared the secret joke with her.

43

Lindsay could tell her brother was starting to get interested in spite of himself, but she was fast losing patience with his subtly patronizing questions.

"One of the guys at work used to race a little," Logan said. "All he'd ever get was a T-shirt and a sunburn, though."

"Logan!" Lindsay spat. "Kit saying he races a little is like IBM saying they make a computer or two. The man has raced in the Tour de France and was on two previous Olympic teams!"

Silence greeted her outraged comment, though all eyes were wide and on Kit. He only shrugged and smiled at her ruefully.

"Wow," Heather breathed, speaking to the whole group for the first time that night, but Lindsay knew it wasn't the first time she'd noticed Kit. Both her and Sue's eyes had been on Kit more than once. She couldn't blame them; a man like Kit naturally drew women's eyes.

Again Lindsay felt empathy for her twin, even though he was acting strangely tonight. For a year and a half—since the beginning of Logan's infatuation with Mara—she'd had trouble understanding how a man like her brother could have fallen so hard for a woman like Mara. Now she knew. It was frighteningly easy.

For her, just watching Kit move was seductive; the play of muscles under his skin was as enticing as the movements of lovers beneath satin sheets. Remembering his kiss made her relax with a sensual lethargy that forced her to lean into Kit for support.

The conversation among the group around the table had resumed, her brother leading it into technical matters that the others jumped at, leaving Lindsay and Kit isolated by the wall of words around them.

"Do you know," Kit said to her, his voice a low murmur. "I don't think your brother likes me. Would you happen to know why?"

Lindsay closed her eyes. When he spoke, she could feel the vibration of his chest against her side, and she wanted him to go on talking just to revel in it. "I think I know why Logan's acting the way he is, which isn't the same thing," she told Kit, matching his low tone. How could she feel so intimately secluded with him in a crowd of people?

"It doesn't matter really. It's his sister who concerns me." He rested his cheek against her hair to bring his lips closer to her ear. "How do you like the race so far?"

"I told you, I'm not a—"

"And don't be fooled by the sedate pace. My specialty is the sprint."

Sedate pace? I thought this *was the sprint!*

Logan's voice interrupted her confusion. "This place is going to close soon. I guess we'd better go on home."

John drove them back to Lindsay's office to drop her and Kit off. She was unpleasantly surprised when Logan hopped out of the van, too, saying Lindsay could drop him off at his house. There was a silent moment between her and her brother when Kit went to get his bicycle to ride home. She knew she was about to find out why he'd been acting strangely toward Kit all evening, and she discovered she didn't want to know.

Kit glided out on his ten-speed, only the subtle clicking of the derailleur sounding in the tense night. Riding up to her, he stopped and put his weight on

45

one foot. The glow from the corner streetlight shadowed his eyes, but she saw him glance once at her brother and then his mouth was on hers in a quick kiss of promise.

His mouth and tongue consumed her lips with a brief taste of banked passion. It was a kiss to challenge her to the race.

"I'll see you on Monday for the second lap," he whispered before riding off into the glowing darkness of a city at night.

CHAPTER THREE

Lindsay whirled on her brother. "Don't say *anything*. Just get in the car."

"Sure, Lin," Logan said sarcastically, his thumb jabbing the chrome button of the Mustang's passenger door handle. "I won't say a thing about my sister picking up a mindless jock or making a fool of herself in front of her friends." He sat down hard on the passenger seat and crossed his arms over his chest uncompromisingly.

"Logan . . ." she said, her voice growling a warning.

"I don't understand you!" Logan cried, hitting his knee with his fist. "A jock! A goddamned fitness freak. You!"

"Kit is not a jock. Sure he's into fitness—he's a world-class cyclist, for God's sake!—but there's more than just muscle between his ears."

"He rides a bike! Normal people stop riding bikes when they learn to drive."

"Stop being so superior. You're certainly not the one to tell me about relationships."

"Mara was a major disaster—we both know that —but because I fell so hard for her, I know how—

how *attractive* people who are physically oriented can be. And how dangerous."

Logan fell silent for a moment, and Lindsay pulled out onto the main street. Though she lived in a condominium only a couple of miles from her office, her brother lived in a house out on Coronado Island. It was a good forty-minute drive round trip, but this drive was going to seem longer than most.

She was angry at his patronizing attitude, but he was her twin and no matter what, they always listened to each other. Because of that she tried to keep the irritation out of her voice. It didn't work.

"I wasn't hiding in a hole somewhere when Mara did her thing. I was right beside you, remember? I managed to learn a thing or two."

He pulled at his left earlobe, a characteristic gesture of frustration that meant he knew he wasn't getting through to her. "But that's it! You think you can approach people like Mara—and this Kit—rationally, logically, as if they were a piece of computer code. But you can't!

"It creeps up on you. It's really—I can't think of the word—having to do with the senses. Suddenly you're aware of how things feel when you touch them, how good someone smells when they've just stepped out of the shower." His eyes focused on the past in the distance. "How sweet it is just to watch her move down the street. . . ." He turned his head away. "But it isn't enough, Lin—for people like us. In the end, it isn't enough."

"Damn it, Loge! I'm twenty-eight! I'm not some fifteen-year-old girl going out on her first date. I'm not stupid. I know what I'm doing with Kit," she said, sounding braver than she felt. His words were hitting all too close to her own doubts.

48

She pulled into his driveway and parked, but he made no move to get out of the car.

"I don't understand you," he said again. "You may be my twin sister, but right now I don't even think we're from the same family. You've only been in that office for two weeks and you've already gone for a guy you *know* is a walking disaster for us.

"Two weeks! After you've managed to completely ignore poor John for years. I think he'll finally give up after your performance tonight."

She certainly wasn't going to tell him his time span was a little off—by about a week and five days. "John gave up years ago. 'Poor John' cares more about that perpetual cold of his than he ever did about me. When he isn't talking about computers, he's talking about cold remedies. His idea of a nightcap is Nyquil on the rocks." She knew she was reacting badly, but he seemed to be goading her into it. "And what do you mean, 'my performance'?"

"Tell me the plot of the movie, sister dear," he said. "When Sue asked you a question about the co-star, you didn't even know what she was talking about! And whispering in the corner of the coffee shop. Tacky, Lin, tacky."

"Tacky? I'll show you tacky—you *deliberately* talked about technical problems you knew Kit couldn't follow. If you were even half as rude to Mara as you were to Kit, it's no wonder she did what she did!"

"If you've got that much sympathy for Mara, why don't you introduce your Kit to *her*. I'm sure they'll have a great time discussing the merits of carrot juice!" Logan grabbed her shoulder. "And the next time you're snuggled up to your muscle man, ask

49

yourself this, Lindsay Trent: is he thinking of you—or your stock dividends?"

Furious, she finally gave free rein to her temper. "You've been making an ass of yourself ever since you laid eyes on Kit tonight," she said. "I don't know why, but I'm sick of it. Now haul yourself out of this car—I'm leaving."

The car door had barely closed when she screeched out of his driveway, leaving long black tread marks on the concrete. Damn him!

The streetlights were turning into bright stars, and she had to close her eyes tight for a second to squeeze out the tears, but she ignored the dampness spilling down her face. For the first time in her life she wished she didn't have a twin; a twin who instinctively knew her fears and didn't hesitate to voice them.

Parking the car in her garage, she bent her head to the steering wheel. She wished, she wished, she wished—she wished Logan weren't so damned *right!*

Early Monday morning she stood in front of her bathroom mirror braiding her hair, pulling the strands tighter than usual. She'd regained most of the equilibrium she had lost in her fight with Logan, but that hadn't kept her from spending the last hour brushing her waist-length hair into different styles.

It had looked rather nice with the top half pulled back into a clip and the rest hanging down her back —at least it had until she remembered that late Sunday afternoon she'd decided to follow Logan's advice and steer clear of Kit; the cyclist would bring her nothing but trouble. The clip had been hastily thrown back into a drawer, and now her customary braid fell to her waist.

Once at the office, she firmly disciplined her mind and worked steadily on her program. She discovered she didn't have to lose her place every time images of a slender, masculine frame intruded on her concentration; she could control her overactive imagination so that even if she couldn't stop thinking about a certain cyclist, at least she didn't keep losing her place in her program logic.

She hunched over the printout on her desk, gnawing on her pencil and idly twisting the tuft of hair at the end of her braid. "That flag is supposed to be set," she muttered to herself. "Why isn't . . . ummm, that could be it." She flipped back through her printout, the rustling of the page masking the faint footsteps on the stairs outside.

"Okay, I give up," Kit said, standing in the doorway waving a manual.

Lindsay tensed for a moment, then dropped her pencil and her braid at the same time. "I beg your pardon? Is something wrong?"

"Oh, no." He walked to her desk and dropped the manual on top of her printout. It was the documentation for his spread-sheet program. "Nothing's wrong. But the score is currently TrentCalc, two; Kit Hawthorne, nothing."

"That bad?" She returned his smile. "Is there something you didn't understand? TCS's documentation is among the best."

He pulled up another chair and sat down. "I'm sure there's not a thing wrong with the manual. My Greek's a little rusty, that's all."

"Aw, c'mon, it's not that hard to understand."

"Harder. I'm going down for the third time," he said, holding his nose and waving three fingers over his head. "You've got to be my lifeguard and save me."

Laughing, Lindsay said, "All right, let's go see what's happening." He grinned.

He whisked her out of her office and down the stairs, and she was only able to wave to Roger before Kit ushered her into his cubbyhole of an office. He followed her in and, to her surprise, shut the door.

Whirling in the confined space, her eyes widened and her brain could think of nothing but a litany of "ohmigod." He smiled mischievously and motioned her to his chair in front of the computer terminal.

Slowly sinking into the chair, she tried to concentrate on remembering the intricacies of the Trent-Calc program, but when Kit pulled up a stool close behind her, her awareness of him overwhelmed her. For a moment she couldn't even read the letters on the terminal screen.

"Did you—did you remember to bring the manual back down?" she stammered. Where were all her cool, rational decisions now?

"It's on the desk," he said, putting his hand on her shoulder nearest the desk. The warmth of his touch remained after she'd retrieved the manual, and she squirmed slightly to try and slough it off. It didn't work. She could feel him watching her, spending an inordinate amount of time studying her close-fitting French T-top. Or maybe he just liked air-brushed unicorns?

Giving herself a mental scold, she called the problem program up; at least it appeared to have been installed right. She was entering one of the simpler commands when she felt him begin to stroke her arm. Starting with short movements, he caressed the rounded cap of her shoulder, then dropped his touch to her upper arm.

Each lengthening stroke sent jolts of a curiously exhilarating energy arcing through her. It felt like desert heat lightning: intense hot fingers of electricity crackling through and around her. Gone was the shelter of her rationalizations about their relationship. She was unprotected and vulnerable on the landscape of her desire.

His other hand slid up and down her side, the heel of his palm slowing each time it traced the swell of her breast. There was no hope of unraveling the program now.

"My Lindsay," he murmured behind her, "my beautiful Lindsay."

She couldn't let herself give in, couldn't let herself slide into the enveloping warmth his caressing hands so sensuously offered. *No!* she wanted to cry, *no, no.* But only the whisper of a sigh escaped.

"Kit, I . . ."

She closed her eyes to concentrate on calming the ragged pulsing in her veins and didn't notice him moving closer until it was too late. He kissed the sensitive skin of her neck where her braid began its dark trail down her back.

Her head fell forward in sacrifice to the demanding ritual of his kisses. Given no quarter by the heat his mouth was breathing into every cell at the base of her neck, she felt a sensual longing well up inside of her as if a new Lindsay were being called into life by his resuscitating kisses.

Kit swiveled the chair, his face close to hers. His lips tasted the soft, creamy skin beneath her ear and the gentle hollow of her cheek before they lowered to cover hers in the softest of tributes. He pulled away,

53

giving her bottom lip a gentle tug. He kissed her again.

Lindsay's body came alive. Never had such flames licked along her veins toward a fire burning in the lower part of her body. His kiss burned away the barriers she'd placed around her passions, unfettering her desire as she had never allowed it to be freed, and she returned his kiss in full measure.

She could hardly recognize the woman who eagerly leaned forward in her chair, letting her hands delight in the feel of the taut undulating muscles at his shoulders. His mouth tasted of apricots, and she found herself wanting to run her tongue along every line of muscle in his body, tasting him completely.

A crashing sound from the shop made them break apart, and Lindsay stared at him, confused and a little appalled at her own part in what had just taken place. But as if sensing her withdrawal, Kit feathered her face with kisses.

"You're like the wildflowers I see along the side of the road when I'm riding," he told her. "Silent and safe in their anonymity, they go unnoticed by passersby—until they bloom."

She could feel small puffs of his breath against her skin as he spoke, making her shiver in response to his intimate closeness.

"You're a wildflower I want to make bloom under my hands, Lindsay, bloom into the passionate woman who's simmering beneath the surface of this soft ivory skin of yours." Kit's lips tasted the corner of her mouth. "I've never known a woman like you—a woman who's so fascinatingly different."

The breath of his words caressed her mouth, and a tiny moan escaped her. Nothing she'd ever experienced had prepared her for this assault on her senses, this floundering in a mass of unfamiliar, irrational emotions. Before she'd met Kit she'd existed in a world of mathematical precision, the days of which followed the logical progression of a computer program.

"Kit," she whispered, hoping to hide the quaver she knew would be in her voice. "Kit, please. This is too fast! You're obviously an expert in the games men and women play. I'm a novice. Don't do this."

He sat back, his hands cradling her face. "It isn't in me to throw the race, Lindsay. But I've never wanted so desperately to win one."

Lindsay pulled back from his touch. "How can you talk like that! You sound as if we've known each other for months instead of days!"

"There was something between us the second you walked in the door—we both know that," he said. "Other people's relationships may start out at a walking pace, but we were in a dead heat from the beginning. And you know it, even if you don't want to admit it."

"I don't believe any such nonsense," she lied.

Smiling, he gently wheeled her chair back to the computer, his hand resting at the base of her neck. "Then you won't mind coming with me on a training ride this weekend. You need some fresh air, and I need someone to cheer me on."

An image of the Amazons she'd seen in his shop flashed through her mind, and she was sure he'd never be short of a cheering section. That thought should have made her want to stay safely in her office, but she found herself accepting his invitation instead. If only he wouldn't touch her like that . . . "All right, I'll go."

"Excellent," he said, drawing her toward him.

He was going to kiss her again, and Lindsay hadn't recovered from the first one. She *had* to get away from this office. Its intimacy only reinforced the tension between them.

Standing suddenly, she broke from his grasp. "I, uh, need to get back to my office," she said quickly, reaching for the doorknob. "I'll see you on Saturday, okay? And I'll check over my TrentCalc manual in the meantime to make sure you're not running into any known glitches. I can't think right now."

His eyes flashed with the green fire of masculine satisfaction.

"I mean I can't think of any bugs in the program right now," she added hastily and fled.

She returned to her office and forced herself to work on her program. It wasn't easy; she couldn't stop thinking of the man or his kiss—or her reaction to it. Surely there was some way to explain away her response, something her mathematically trained mind could understand.

But Logan's words came back to mock her. "You think you can approach people like Mara—and this Kit—rationally, logically, as if they were a piece of computer code. But you can't!" The last words echoed in her brain: "You can't!" But she had to! It was either that or fall victim to a bigger disaster than the one that befell Logan.

She sat in front of her terminal, listening to the hums and whirs of the computer while it assembled her program for the umpteenth time.

When it was done assembling, she link-loaded it and waited for the command file to be formed. That done, she typed in the command name she'd given it and, crossing her fingers, hit the return key.

The computer hummed contentedly for a while,

then stopped, the program obviously sending it off into never-never land.

"Damn it! Why the hell won't it work? I've checked it over and over and over and I still get nothing," she said, rubbing her face in exasperation. "Why is the damn thing hanging up!" Unconsciously her hand formed a fist, and it came down hard onto the keyboard.

The violence of what she'd done shocked her. Covering her face with her hands, she wilted in her chair and bent until her forehead touched her knees. She *had* to come to grips with what was happening to her! What could she do? She was in the middle of a tug-of-war, her mind pulling her away from him, and her body—warm with the memory of his kiss—urging her into his arms.

She popped the program disk out and filed it; she didn't even want to *see* that particular piece of code for a good long while. Flipping through the other disks, her fingers lighted on Timecast, and she faltered. It was the game she'd written that Roger enjoyed so much—and the one Kit had asked her about.

A sense of perversity made her jam the disk in the drive. "At least *this* works," she said, calling up the game. It had been a while since she'd played it herself, but between what had happened in Kit's office and her program bombing, she needed to do something to restore her confidence. The copyright notice flashed by and she smiled.

"Ah-h-h-h, there we go." The words scrolled onto the screen: "You're in a meadow surrounded by wildflowers." Her heart jumped at those words. Kit had called her a wildflower. Shaking her head to clear it, she continued reading.

"To the north is a swiftly flowing river, to the south is a dense forest. Nearby is a ring of stones that appears to be shimmering in the heat.

"There is a knife encrusted with jewels here.

"There is an empty canteen here.

"There is a knapsack here.

"There is a Roman coin here."

She giggled and typed in the words: "Get knife."

Three hours later she was stuck in the dungeon of Vlad the Terrible's castle. There was supposed to be a secret passage out of it, but she couldn't remember where it was and she was getting frustrated. As a ruse to help her put Kit from her mind, the game was a partial success, but she was failing miserably at improving her temper. The manacles on the wall were the only thing she hadn't tried yet, so she typed in "Yank chain."

The computer responded with: "I don't know that word."

"What do you mean, you don't know that word?" she shouted at the computer. "Of course you know it, you stupid parser, I *wrote* you!" She determinedly started to type the command in again. "Yank . . ."

"Now, now," Kit said, coming up behind her. "You shouldn't be that upset at your own creation. It reflects on you—and no one could ever call you stupid."

Lindsay spun and watched him warily, ignoring his words. She glanced at the open door behind her and frowned. A nice, loud bell was going to be added to her list of office supplies.

He studied the terminal screen for a moment. "Is

it the parser that told you it didn't understand what you'd typed?"

She almost forgot her bad mood and smiled. He caught on to her world quickly. "You're close," she said. "Actually it's the structure that interprets character strings. When the parser can't match a word that's been typed in with a word in its list, it branches to another program and prints 'I don't know that word' on the screen."

Sighing, she deleted what she'd started to type onto the screen. "I'd forgotten how frustrating it can be to keep running into that silly phrase over and over again."

She quit the game and put the disk away. There wasn't any use in even trying to play with Kit nearby. She could feel her nerves beginning to react to him; he was like a fire on a cold winter night: warm and inviting, but if she stood too close, she'd get burned.

"You didn't have to quit on my account." He kneeled to pick up a book she'd thrown onto the floor when she'd been working on her assembly language program. "Heavy stuff," he said, reading the title of an assembly language reference work. "Do you have to know all this to be able to program?"

"No, not really," she answered. He was stalling, and she knew it. "That's more for fancy code and complex programming." She watched him replace the book and reach for another one. "What is it you want, Kit?"

He let his eyes travel slowly over her; it was a long minute before his eyes met hers again and he smiled. "A favor. I went down when I was coming back from lunch and—"

"Are you all right?" Lindsay interrupted. A jolt of terror hit her when she realized that the mild, euphe-

59

mistic phrase "went down" meant he'd crashed. Without thinking she rose and went to him. "My God! You could have been killed! Did you go to a doctor? Have some X rays taken?"

His eyes lit with pleasure at her concern, and he gently gripped her shoulders. "No, no, I'm fine— really. I've gone down before and no doubt will again. And I always wear a helmet."

Kit placed a light kiss on her forehead, and a frisson of pleasure went through her, melting all her mental scoldings and resolutions like a castle of sand at high tide. She *had* to tell him it would never work between them. His hands gently kneaded her shoulders, and it took her a moment to remember what she'd just decided.

"The problem is that I've been too swamped to check out the frame. I can't use it if it was bent and I need to get home early tonight. Can you give me a ride?"

"Of course, Kit," she said, stepping back. "Let me finish up here; then we can go." She shut the computer systems off, and the sudden quiet revealed a disturbing intimacy between them.

The feeling didn't dissipate as they drove out of the parking lot and headed west on Garnet. A short while later she was easing into his driveway. His house was only a few blocks from her condo. It was set sideways on a hill and had been built on three levels. The part of the backyard she could see looked unique, with a swimming pool adjacent to the lowest level and a sun deck over one end off the second level.

"Why don't you come in and have a drink to cool off," he said. "Only take a minute."

Lindsay started to decline, but she knew so little

about him that her curiosity overrode her caution and she agreed.

A quick glass of iced tea—and that's all! she told herself as he led her inside. But she wasn't prepared for the spectacular view of the Pacific through sliding glass doors leading out to the wooden deck or the delicious smell she inhaled when she entered his house on the middle level.

"That smells wonderful!"

He bent slightly at the waist in a teasing bow and said, "Thank you, my love. That's Hawthorne's Special Marinara Sauce." He escorted her into the kitchen and opened the oven door, letting delicious smells escape into the room.

Retrieving a mysterious jar from his refrigerator, he said, "I just have to add the last secret ingredient and let it simmer for twenty more minutes, then it'll be ready. Why don't you stay and have a taste?"

He closed the oven door and, leaning against the smooth butcher-block counter, challenged her with an uncompromising gaze. Alarms clamored in her brain—she had to leave *now*! But he obviously understood her feelings, and the challenge in his eyes told her even if she ran tonight, the race would still be on.

Sometime soon he was going to have to realize there was more to Lindsay Trent than a suddenly overactive, libidinous imagination. And that time might as well be tonight. Taking a deep breath, she said, "Sure. That smells too delicious to pass up."

He poured her a glass of iced sun tea and led her to a rocking chair in the living room. She settled back, expecting him to sit down in the chair next to hers, and was surprised when he remained standing. "I'll be back in a few minutes. Someone's picking me

61

up in about an hour for a meeting tonight, so I need to get ready to go."

"Why didn't you say so? I should leave right now," she said, rising from the chair and setting her glass on a nearby table.

His hands gently pressed her back into the seat. "And miss a taste of Hawthorne's specialty?" He kneeled beside her and drew her toward him. His mouth pulled tenderly at her lips, kissing her with a seductive tug that told her how much he wanted to savor all of her in that same way.

He stood slowly, his hand smoothing the wispy strands of her dark hair. "I think my shower had better be a cold one." And with a light kiss on the top of her head, he left.

Thank God he has to go to a meeting. She leaned back into the soft cushions of the chair and concentrated on the muted sound of the running water of Kit's shower. Closing her eyes in a feeble attempt to ward off the now-familiar reactions, she tried to relax.

If she had a computer with this many unpredictable responses, she'd have junked the thing in a minute. But she wasn't a computer—not even close—as Kit was proving all too clearly.

The telephone rang, interrupting her none-too-calming line of thinking. Over the sound of his shower, she heard Kit shout for her to answer it.

Wearing a dark green robe and toweling his hair, he walked into the room as she hung up the receiver. "Is something wrong?" he asked. "You look scared."

"No, nothing's wrong," she said, trying desperately to keep her panic in check. When he'd walked into the room, her impulse had been to run to him and revel in the touch of the shower-warmed flesh be-

62

neath his robe. The effort to control herself left her shaken. "That was Steve from your University Avenue store. He said to tell you tonight's meeting has been canceled."

Now what was she going to do? The meeting had been the last safeguard against her own desire. She watched him drape the towel around his neck and run his fingers through his pale hair to try to give it some order. The tanned V of his chest exposed by the robe glowed golden in the rose light of dusk coming through the sliding glass doors, giving him a look of an aureate fire.

Forcing her eyes to the sunset, she saw the sun melt into a pool of gold at the edge of the Pacific. The fading liquid sunlight dazzled her eyes, but its glare couldn't burn out the one truth she wanted obliterated.

She wanted Kit. She desired him more than she had ever desired a man before, and she knew he wanted her. There was no hope for them. That was unarguable, but she would soon be swept up by the brief solar flare of passion and consumed by the bright burning pain of that passion's death unless she left. *Now.*

He came up behind her and circled her waist with his arms. Drawing her back to rest against his fresh, moist warmth, he said softly, "Stay for dinner. Then you'll get more than just a taste of my specialty."

If she didn't leave now, there would be no turning back.

"I'll stay."

CHAPTER FOUR

"What do you think of my specialty?" Kit asked after the meal. They were outside, leaning against the deck's railing, sipping a California Johannesburg Riesling for dessert and enjoying the night. The moon hadn't risen yet, and the world glowed with the sapphire of twilight, making the swimming pool below them gleam like a brilliant gem set in the earth.

"Fishing for compliments?" she said, laughing. "You know it was superb. How did you ever learn to cook like that? My culinary skill is limited to programming my microwave to heat up frozen entrées."

"Are you sure you don't want to sneak out to McDonald's and get a burger fix?" His words were light, but something in his tone told her he would take her answer seriously.

She smiled and shook her head. "Not at all." Letting him refill her wineglass, she added, "I have to admit I was surprised tonight. I'd written off last Saturday's lunch as a delicious fluke. To me being a vegetarian meant eating beans and brown rice, sometimes with tofu on the side. It certainly didn't mean fresh homemade pasta with a glorious marinara sauce."

Kit took a long sip of his wine. "Thank you for saying that, Lindsay."

There was silence then as darkness overtook the night like a dream. But the somnolence around her made her own agitation stand out sharp and clear. Her opinion of him and his life-style mattered to him, and that bothered her. It wasn't supposed to matter, because if it did, they were both headed for disaster.

Lindsay finished her wine and Kit took her glass, setting both his and hers on the small redwood table nearby. She'd expected him to do or say something, but he only mimicked her pose by leaning on the railing with his elbows and said nothing.

Their arms were close on the railing, and she could sense the nearness of him all along her body, feel the tenseness between them as if they'd been caught at the edge of a thunderstorm about to break.

How could the spring night be so calm and cool when such a devastating tropical storm named Kit stood next to her? She could feel the winds of her own suppressed desire whipping at her, weakening her resolve and making her tremble with the gale force of her passion.

"Are you cold?" He straightened and reached out to put his arm around her shoulder, but at the last minute he seemed to catch himself and merely gestured toward the open sliding glass door. "My mind was . . . wandering," he said, his eyes traveling over her with barely suppressed hunger. Taking a deep lungful of air, he added, "Let's go inside. It'll be warmer for you."

Warmer? Warmth was the last thing she needed, considering that if her body temperature rose any higher, it'd have to be measured in degrees Kelvin.

He followed her back into his living room, surprising her when he still didn't try to touch her. Relaxing with the mistaken notion that if he kept his distance, the tempest raging within her would lessen and disappear, Lindsay sat in a huge recliner.

She tried to sit back in it, but the slightest pressure on the arms made the chair tilt back quickly, and she found herself staring at the ceiling. A chuckle from her right made her turn her head.

Her gaze met strong, muscled thighs encased in faded jeans. The material had softened with time and fit his legs almost as closely as his skin shorts had. Her pulse jumped. Disconcerted by the sudden prickles of heat deep within her, she moved her eyes upward to escape the visual temptation, only to encounter his slim hips and the tantalizing swell of his jeans.

"I forgot to warn you about the chair," he said, his words giving her the impetus to look up at his face. "Let me help you up."

Evidently her reaction had taken only seconds instead of the minutes it had seemed, and he hadn't noticed the direction of her fascinated gaze. She felt the chair tip forward when he pushed it from the back and she gratefully started to sit upright again.

"Ouch!"

"What's wrong?" he asked anxiously, kneeling next to her. He grabbed her hand and began massaging it before she could answer. "You didn't pinch a finger, did you?"

"My hand's fine," she said, her head tilted at an odd angle. "It's my braid. It's caught."

"Let me tilt the chair back again and you can pull it out, okay?"

She tried to nod, but her captured hair prevented her. "Fine."

When it was free, he gently draped it over her shoulder. "I hope it didn't hurt you too much." He sat on the arm of the chair and slowly massaged the back of her neck.

Several long minutes passed in silence until his fingers began to trace the intricacies of the dark plait, following the path of the thick strand down her shoulder. She held her breath when his touch slowed its path over her braid where it fell across the swell of her breast. Suddenly she realized his hand was descending to where the thick tuft of hair at the end of the plait rested in her lap.

Lindsay had never felt that kind of tension rippling under the surface of her body. The blood in her veins was pumping in rhythm to his short, slow strokes; she consciously had to make her lungs fill with air. What would happen if he touched her? What would happen when he reached the junction of her thighs where the end of her braid had fallen?

His hand flattened as it crossed the soft planes of her stomach. His voice was a broken whisper when he said, "You're a fantasy come to life." The descent of his hand stopped and he reverently lifted the plait of her hair. Kissing the dark sable strands, he murmured, "A fascinating . . . tantalizing . . . woman."

Hunger for her flashed through his eyes like sunlight cutting through the dark verdure of a forest. Without saying anything more, he grasped the rubber band that held her hair and tugged.

It had been wrapped around several times. Their gazes locked, he slowly tugged off each layer with excruciating slowness. The simple act was intimate and arousing, as if it were her clothes he was removing and not merely the rubber band from her hair.

And though her uneven breathing was the only sound in the room, she somehow realized his athlete's trained body had had to take over to control his own erratic breathing.

When the braid's restraint was at last removed and discarded, she felt freed from all the restraints Lindsay Trent had wound around herself. Kit's eyes never left hers, making her admit that the restraints had been discarded when she'd agreed to stay for dinner.

Her gaze dropped to his hands. He was undoing her braid, carefully parting each bundle of deep brown satin. His fingers buried themselves within each V of hair and then pulled them apart. It was impossible to watch the sensual grace of his movements and not wonder what it would feel like on her skin.

Through the haze of passion he was weaving around them as he unwove her braid, she noticed an odd melting sensation at the seat of her desire. How could she feel such a need for him when he'd barely touched her? As he undid her hair, tiny hairs were pulled, not hurting her but making her tremble with that barely leashed need.

She couldn't help it. When he reached the nape of her neck to finished unbraiding her hair, her eyes closed of their own accord and her head fell forward.

Then there was stillness. She opened her eyes and watched him as he consumed the sight of her with her hair spread across the front of her body like a sable fan.

He groaned and slid against the chair's leather to

wedge in next to her, her body molding to his contours.

"Kit," she breathed. Truth and desire mingled to make her add, "I need you. Please."

"Lin, are you sure?" he whispered. "I need you so badly I ache with it."

He kissed her hair and said, "I know I should've tried to slow down what was happening between us, but everything about you only makes me want you more." He punctuated his words with kisses; tender, gentle tributes that made her ache for him.

The chair started to tip back of its own accord, but he stopped it, then stood and held out his hands to Lindsay.

Without a thought for anything but the urging within her and the green eyes intently looking down into hers, she held out her hands and was pulled into his arms.

He kissed her deeply, letting his lips and tongue show her he would accept nothing less than complete participation. Each quick thrust into the sweet interior of her mouth, each savoring taste of the tender pinkness of her lips demanded that she return his kiss in full measure. And she did.

The analytical part of her mind slid away like a hidden door opening to reveal the precious treasures of the human heart, the desire to accept all of the bequest of her humanity—not only the portion that gave her her intellect, but the part that let her give and receive pleasure and reach the heights only such sharing can attain.

Kit buried his face in her hair. She thought she heard him murmur, "Glorious, glorious," but she wasn't sure; she was too busy reveling in the feel of the movement of his muscles.

69

He picked her up, watching the fall of her hair across his shoulder and down her back. Carrying her up the short flight of stairs to his bedroom, he radiated strength and power, and she was almost overwhelmed with the need to be suffused by that power.

She saw only the man whose slightest movement mesmerized her and very little of the blue, brown and cream tones of the room. Kit turned Lindsay into kindling, making tiny flames lick along her veins to gather into a deep-seated fire. Her emotions danced in the waves of heat atop that fire, and when he lowered her to the bed, she didn't immediately notice that it danced with her.

"Kit?" she murmured.

"It's all right, my love," he assured her while getting rid of their cumbersome clothes. "It's just a water bed."

"Mmmm," she answered, already forgetting that the soft sheet beneath echoed her movements. Kit's hands slid over her skin with abandon, each long stroke like a deep drink of water to a parched man.

Her own hands splayed across his chest, his slender but tautly muscled body fascinating her. Was the woman reveling so freely in this masculine body really Lindsay Trent? The Lindsay she remembered never had such an elemental heat urging her to touch, to kiss, to fulfill. The Lindsay she remembered had never wanted to feel the primal power of a man so completely.

"Kit, please," she whimpered, not caring that she so blatantly told him of her need. "Please . . ."

"I want it to be good for you, my Lin-love," he told her. "So good."

His lips nipped at the base of her breasts, his tongue flicking out to taste her sweetness. When his lips traveled up the mound of her breast to tease and pull at the rose-colored peak, she was hardly aware of the moan that escaped her as she writhed beneath him.

How could she continue to breathe with this ache inside her? How could her heart continue to beat so furiously for so long? But Kit would not give her surcease.

His devastating mouth moved to the other peak, then slowly descended to her almond-shaped navel, where his active tongue zigzagged along its rim. He went farther still and traced the outline of her soft, sable triangle with kisses. Reaching the apex, his hands slid beneath her and pulled her upward to his waiting lips.

"Kit!" she cried when he kissed her there. "Kit! *Christopher!*"

Then his body hovered over hers and he kissed her with a hard, demanding kiss, and she answered it with demands of her own.

He lowered his hips toward her, and feeling the searing heat of his male need against her thigh, her hips rose instinctively to meet him. The white-hot path traveled up to the very center of her womanhood, and she unconsciously held her breath, waiting.

A cry of joy escaped her when she felt him slide into her. Nothing could be more exquisite than the sensation of having him in her; it was such a warm sense of completion in itself that she was slightly surprised when he began moving his hips in a slow rhythm.

With the intuition of passion, she moved with him, and the bed echoed their movements with sensual undulation. He was taking her higher than she'd ever been before, and the progression was calling forth a greater response than she'd thought herself capable of giving. At the core of her flame, muscles tightened and released with the rhythm of a woman's deepest passion.

Kit moaned, and his thrusts increased in tempo. In seconds a cry broke from her as she reached the precipice and exploded into a thousand fragments of spinning light. She had barely returned when he followed her to the heights and a deep, primal sound was wrenched from him.

Covered with a sheen of perspiration, they both lay panting for long minutes. When their breathing had returned to near normal, Kit propped himself up on one elbow.

He kissed her reverently and drew her into his arms to sleep.

Something was pulling at her head. "Hmmphf?" Mornings were not Lindsay's strong suit, and it took another tug to make her turn over. Something beneath her rocked her gently. Throwing her arm across her eyes to shield them from the dim light, she tried to recapture the warm sense of contentment she remembered from her dream.

"Go back to sleep," a deep masculine voice whispered.

What a nice voice; it sounded like Kit's. *Kit.* She peeked out from under her arm to see a golden expanse of naked male bending to put on a pair of shorts.

"Is something wrong?" she asked groggily. "What time is it?"

He kneeled on the bed and kissed her between her breasts. "It's five-thirty. Now go back to sleep."

Quickly covering herself with a sheet, she said, "Five-thirty! Is the house on fire?" Why else would he be getting up at such an hour?

The sound of his soft laugh caressed her. "No," he said. "It's just time for me to work out. I'm sorry I disturbed you."

She moved to the edge of the bed and sat up, the movement punctuated with a huge yawn. "Do you always get up this early?"

"Only when I'm in training for a race."

"What race?" she asked, yawning again.

"It's a road race called El Diablo del Sol—the Sun Devil." He dropped a kiss on her forehead. "Now go back to sleep."

A few minutes later she heard the subtle metal sound of clicking weights coming from the lower floor. Intrigued, she donned the robe she found hanging on the back of the bathroom door and headed in the direction of the steady beats.

Lindsay stopped in the doorway to his "gym" and gaped. Expecting a modest layout, she was stunned by the gleaming Nautilus equipment set at intervals around the room. It was a complete professional gym. In addition to the sauna in one corner, she could see a whirlpool outside on the patio next to the swimming pool. He certainly believed in getting the best.

"Feel free to go get some breakfast," he said between controlled breaths as he lifted a bar attached to weights. "I'll join you in about half an hour."

Pulling his robe around her tightly, she watched the muscles flow under his skin and remembered how those same bands of male steel had felt under her hands the night before.

What had happened? What would happen? She

73

could barely think, but somehow it didn't seem necessary at that moment to think at all—only to enjoy the sight of the man she cared for.

"We'll have to stop by my place for me to get some clothes," she told him, and he nodded.

"No problem."

Kit followed her into her condominium. After eating her modest attempt at an omelet with flattering relish, he'd foregone his usual twenty-five-mile morning ride and accompanied her here.

Nervously removing a stack of old *Byte* magazines from the sofa, she motioned to him to sit down. "Let me take a quick shower and then we can go, okay?"

He smiled and started flipping through one of the magazines.

She didn't take long and was soon walking back into the living room. He looked up, and his pleasant greeting stumbled to a halt.

"That was qui . . ." His eyes widened and he stood, staring at her. "It's even more beautiful than I remembered."

She watched him shyly as he walked toward her. Her newly washed hair was still too damp to put into a braid and it hung naturally in a cascade that fell past her waist. His arms went around her, and he buried his hands in the satiny mass.

"Can you be real?" he murmured, placing tiny kisses along her hairline. "Can a man really be so lucky as to feel his dreams alive in his arms?" He kissed her neck and behind her ear, burying his face in her hair. "You smell so *good*. The fragrance of my woman just out of the shower. No perfume could come close."

Why did she think of Logan right then? At least

now she understood what Logan had been talking about. She felt as if all the glory and wonder in the world was shared with a caress. When Kit's lips suddenly descended on hers, Lindsay met them willingly, and together they wove a spell of desire. She always wanted to remember what it felt like to be touched by magic.

His tongue plunged into her mouth, and she instinctively drew it in farther with her own spiraling need. A moan escaped him, feeding her passion, and she deepened the kiss.

But a cry came from the deep hidden place in her mind where the analytical Lindsay had flown, a cry for survival. It startled her, breaking the enchantment of their desire.

When they broke apart, he cupped her face with his hands and she could feel his uneven breath on her face when he said, "My Lindsay, I never guessed you would be the race of my life. Sh-h-h-h. No, you don't have to tell me I have a long way to go before I've truly won."

He had more than a long way to go; he had to cross the infinite gulf between their life-styles, and she knew it would never be. Smiling shakily, she removed his hands. "We should be going or you'll be late."

Lindsay hoped the cool morning air on the drive to their office building would help calm the intensity between them. But Kit sat in the passenger seat idly playing with her hair, stroking it, drawing his hand through it as if mesmerized.

Desperately trying to control the pleasure she felt at his touch, she said, "Why do you work out so hard? It looked almost painful."

He smiled. "Fitness is important to me. I'm a very

75

physical person. Even when I was a kid and still riding an old balloon-tire coaster-brake bike, I felt more comfortable with things I could see and feel and experience."

He was silent while she maneuvered into the parking lot at their building. When she'd parked, he turned in his seat and added, "I guess you could say I prefer realities to abstractions. And sometimes reality can be beautiful."

His index finger traced her profile, then tilted her face toward his and kissed her gently.

Slowly mounting the stairs, she wondered at her own stupidity. His words had only pointed up the incredible differences between them. Her world was built on abstractions, his on the concrete.

How could she even consider that a computer freak whose idea of exercise was running through a mathematical equation could *ever* be compatible with a vegetarian cyclist into physical fitness? It was absurd; yet there had been nothing absurd about the night before. Just remembering the sound of their labored breathing in the still night affected her.

Stifling a cough, she dug out the problem assembly program and started working on it. She wasn't feeling very well this morning and no doubt that was making everything seem bleaker than it was.

The bugs in her program turned out to be fairly minor ones and, shaking her head over her earlier frustration, she fixed them quickly. That was the difficult part about programming: One innocuous little instruction in the wrong place could wreak monumental havoc.

Her cough progressively worsened during the day. By the time her brother called, she couldn't say a complete sentence without interrupting it with a rasping cough.

"I wanted to apologize for what I said the other night," Logan said. "I suppose I overreacted. It's just that this Kit fellow is the *last* kind of guy I expected you to fall for. But you've got plenty of good sense, Lin, and I know you'll come out okay. I love you, but you already know that."

"I know it, Logan," she said, "I know." Though her cough hadn't improved, she felt much better and assured him she'd be fine in a day or two.

By the middle of the afternoon her cough was being accompanied by sneezing fits, and she decided to call it quits. Her program was running well and only needed some fine tuning, so it was a good time to get away.

Remembering that Kit hadn't ridden his bicycle in that day, she stopped off at his shop to see if he was going to need a ride home. The place was crowded with cyclists, all evidently getting ready for the training ride that coming weekend, but that didn't stop Kit from greeting her with a devastating smile.

That smile and his introduction of her as his computer expert made more than one pair of eyes stare at her with open curiosity. Leaving Roger in charge for a few minutes, Kit whisked her off into his office, where he indulged in a more private greeting and kissed her.

While his lips teased and caressed her mouth with pleasant abandon, his hands stroked her hair lovingly.

"I stopped by to see if you need a ride home," she said breathily. She licked her lips, wondering how a man could taste so good. If the seasons could be sampled, his kisses would be like spring, when everything was fresh and wondrous and newly alive.

Rubbing her shoulders, he said, "Thanks, Lin-love, but Steve's picking me up. That meeting's been rescheduled for tonight." He kissed her again. "But will you have dinner with me tomorrow night?"

"More specialties?" she teased.

"Of course. I have a very extensive repertoire," he said with a grin. "It's going to take a long time to sample everything."

His head lowered for another kiss, but she had to step back quickly and cough. "Excuse me. It must be some early summer allergy."

"Sure you're okay?"

"Fine." Her eyes swept over his face. "Kit," she said hesitantly, "why do you call me Lin-love? You . . . you used it last night, too." The recollection of *when* he'd used it made a blush steal up her cheeks.

His smile was slow and sensual. "Ask me again the next time we're alone—really alone. I'll give you a full explanation."

That night she was still thinking of his provocative answer.

By noon the next day her coughing and sneezing had worsened, and she finally had to admit she had a cold. Sighing, she sat back in her chair and stared at the computer screen. *Just what I don't need.* She'd wanted to start extensive testing of her program, but her mouth tasted like the stuffing inside a mailing bag and her brain was starting to act like her mouth felt.

She looked through the open doorway to the bright sunshine outside and grimaced. Naturally she had to feel rotten on a perfectly gorgeous day. Logan walked in while she was still staring blankly out the door.

"I was going to ask if you feel any better," he said, "but I can see you don't." John and Heather followed him into the room, and Lindsay had to stifle a groan. She did not feel like dealing with a crowd at the moment.

John, she thought. "You! You gave me this cold," she accused, pointing at him and swiveling in her chair to follow him as he carried something to her kitchenette. He set it down with a plunk. "After six years of immunity, why did you have to be infectious *now*?"

He sneezed, and she echoed it with a sneeze of her own. When Logan started to chuckle, she whirled on him. "Don't you dare laugh. I am not in a good mood." A ragged indrawn breath turned into a coughing fit, and it was several minutes before she could add, "This is going to put me even further behind schedule with that wretched program."

"Now, Lin. John felt so bad when I told him about your cold, he fixed up his best cure for you and rushed it down here," Logan said, indicating the large pump Thermos setting on the counter. He gave John an odd look. "He assures me you'll feel better right away."

"Thank you," she said with mock graciousness. Since John had given her the cold in the first place, the least he could do was try to cure it with one of his famous remedies.

She hated taking medicine of any kind, so for several hours she only glowered at the Thermos whenever a sneezing or coughing fit seized her. But after a particularly rough spasm, she decided a small dose couldn't hurt.

Pushing down on the top of the Thermos, she put a little in the bottom of one of the paper cups John had brought and swished it around. She sighed in relief and downed the cold liquid in one swallow. It was only lemonade.

At least it was something Kit would approve of. The thought was inexplicably cheering, and she filled the cup again. It was tasty, or at least she thought it was, but since her taste buds had died several hours back, she couldn't be sure. She couldn't smell it, either, which was a pity, because she'd always enjoyed that biting citrusy aroma. Not that it mattered, of course. It only had to work.

She measured out another cupful, and another, then swallowed experimentally; it did seem to be easier.

Walking back to her terminal, she frowned at the screen. "Bah! Who wants to work on that boring old thing." She popped the disk out of the drive and giggled when it shot into her waiting hand. "Steeee-rike one!"

After putting the disk away she laughed and rolled her chair around on the acrylic floor mat. She certainly was feeling better. A particularly vigorous spin made her dizzy and she stopped for a minute, draping her arm over the nearest computer to rest.

Another computer sitting next to the wall caught her attention, and her eyes narrowed. It was model five-twenty—one of the first TCS had put out—and geared to the home arcade-game market. It had been upgraded considerably since then, but Lindsay had always had a sentimental attachment to the old original.

Stopping at the Thermos for another couple of doses of lemonade, she sat down in front of the five-twenty. How long had it been since she'd played a really good, old-fashioned ack-ack-gun arcade game? Too long! Grabbing a game cartridge with Yart March written in flaming hot pink across the top, she popped it in and hit the start button.

"Okay, all you Yarts—prepare to die!"

It was nearing five when Kit walked in and found her still playing the game. "Lindsay, are you ready to—" he began. Hearing her make machine-gun noises had halted him in his tracks. "What are you doing?"

"Saving the world for democracy," she cried. "Ka-*pow*! Take that!"

"Lindsay, what about your cold?"

"My cold? What—Oh, Kit! Hi," she said, none too coherently. She jumped up and ran to him, throwing her arms around his neck and kissing him with a loud smack. "Hi! I got seventy-eight thousand points and blasted away *three* Head Yarts! Not bad for someone who's rusty, eh?"

She nuzzled his neck and said in a low, throaty voice, "And how many points would *you* give me to blast away your . . ." She paused, slid her hand under his shirt and lightly scratched a trail down his back. "Yarts." Feeling a shiver pass through him, she smiled slyly and took tiny nips at his neck with her teeth.

He took a deep breath and unwound her arms from his neck. Holding her a safe distance away, he said in a slightly shaky voice, "Your cold, Lindsay. How are you feeling?"

She broke his light hold on her hands and wrapped her arms around him again. "I feel won-der-ful," she said, slipping the last syllable over her bottom lip.

Giggling, she added, "Now let's rack up some points."

"Lindsay, did you take something for your cold?" Kit asked, half-laughing as he tried to stop her hands from roaming under his shirt again.

Grinning wickedly, she waved toward the Thermos resting on the kitchenette counter. "Sure did. Best little ol' cure north of the border." When he raised his head to look, she found the opening she'd been waiting for and buried her head in his neck, licking, sucking and kissing the sensitive skin there. She felt another shiver go through him, and her arms tightened their hold.

"Lindsay. Lindsay! Honey, wait a minute, I want to check that 'cure' of yours." He finally managed to unwind her. "Now stay here. No! No, I don't need a good-bye kiss, I'm only going to walk over to the counter."

He poured out the last few ounces and tasted it. "Good God. No wonder—"

She tiptoed up behind him and twined her arms around his waist. Her fingers slid under his blue-striped shirt again and stroked a long, sensuous path on his flat stomach and chest while her hips curved and undulated against his tight round buttocks.

"Lindsay," he gasped in a hoarse whisper. He disentangled her once again and cleared his throat. "Where did you—Lindsay, where did you get this stuff?"

She'd started toward him again, but his words had forestalled her and she contented herself with tracing the outline of the hand grasping the cup he held out to her. "Oh, John brought it by. What's it matter? It's only lemonade."

"*Lemonade?*" He pulled his hand away and set the

cup on the counter. "Honey, this kind of lemonade is sold in large round glasses with salt on the rim. You've had the equivalent of about four *generous* Margaritas."

She shrugged and slipped a hand around his back. When he was occupied with trying to remove that hand, she closed in from the front and, pulling up his shirt, began taking tiny nips along the faint line of his ribs.

He sucked in his breath and a groan escaped before he managed to grasp her shoulders and hold her away from him.

"Lindsay, honey—"

But she wasn't listening. She used the opportunity to unbutton his shirt, her insatiable lips darting in and kissing and licking his flat male nipples. His breath came in shorter and shorter gasps until he leaned back against the counter as if to steady himself.

"Honey, you don't understand. You're dru—" His voice faltered when she drew her tongue along the outline of his pectorals. "Lin," he said with a groan.

Pushing his shirt down his arms, she feasted on his smooth golden chest while her hands hungered to feel every inch of him. She uttered a cry of delight when she discovered tiny white blond hairs leading down from his navel to disappear tantalizingly beneath the waistband of his jeans, and she pulled at them sensually with her lips. He trembled.

"Honey, please—" Taking a deep breath, he shrugged his shirt back onto his shoulders and held her from him. "Lindsay, listen to me. You're drunk. You don't know what you're doing."

She giggled. "Oh, I don't? Then I'll have to figure it out, won't I?"

Her hands slid up his chest to meet at the base of his neck and run her fingers through his hair. She tilted his head toward hers and kissed him, playfully moving her moist lips over his before her own need compelled her to press harder into his mouth. Feeling him respond, she thrust in her tongue to search the hidden slick interior.

Weakened barriers fell aside and she felt the full force of her urgent desire. The persuasive memories of his lovemaking drove her to seek that complete fulfillment in his arms. She deepened the kiss.

As if of their own accord, his hands clasped her waist and drew her closer. She moaned her approval and her hips, the seat of her consuming need, slowly ground against the swelling mound in his jeans.

His hands held her face and he broke away. After taking several deep breaths, he said raggedly, "I need to take you home. You need—we *both* need some fresh air."

"I can breathe fine in here," she said.

Taking another deep breath, he said, "But honey, *I* can't. And you should be home in bed."

A wide smile lit her face.

"*Asleep,* Lindsay," Kit said. "You need to recover."

With a disappointed shrug she let him lock her office. She reluctantly handed him the car keys and got in the passenger side. A few seconds later she brightened when she noticed how intimate a car's interior could be.

She had a marvelous time on the ride home, and by the time they pulled into her driveway, she had her own plans for recovery. Only this time she didn't need a Thermos bottle; her cure stood six feet tall and weighed about a hundred sixty pounds.

"You go on in," he said in a tight voice. "I'll be along in a minute."

"Ah, c'mon! I want to show you something."

"In a minute. Go on, now." He gripped the steering wheel as he tried to control his breathing.

"Why won't you come in now?" she asked. "Are you angry with me?"

He laughed ruefully. "No, you little witch, I am not angry with you. I'm not getting out of the car because I *can't.*"

A quick glance at his lap confirmed her suspicions, and she had to stifle a giggle. "Oh, Kit, I'm sorry. I didn't realize . . ." But seeing how much he wanted her made her even more determined. Her fingers traced idle patterns on his neck just inside his collar. "I'll wait for you."

He shook his head and leaned slightly forward. "I don't think that'll work."

"Oh, all right. I'll go," she said with a pout. "But I really do have something to show you."

He nodded.

The minute she entered her living room, she went to the corner dominated by a computer and picked up the phone. After quickly connecting to an on-line computer service and selecting Sports Facts, she soon found what she had discovered the night before —the listing of Kit's statistics.

He walked into the house, and she motioned him over to the corner. "Here, this is what I wanted to show you." She pointed to the left-hand column on the screen. "See there? 'Christopher Nathaniel Hawthorne, thirty-four. San Diego, California.' "

She gave him her seat and let him read through the stats. Though her nose was still stuffy, her discomfort had been completely overrun by the urgings of desire. Standing behind him, her hands slid around his neck and her index finger trailed across the tanned V his shirt revealed. He gave a mock sigh and sat back, a smile hovering on his lips.

"You make it very difficult for a man to concentrate," he said, swiveling the chair to face her.

"That's the idea," she said with a laugh. Suddenly she kneeled in front of him, her hands already busy unbuttoning his shirt. She kissed the slight protrusion of his Adam's apple and nibbled along his collarbone.

His hands strayed to her sides. "Lindsay, you need to rest. You may only have a slight cold now, but if you don't take care of it, it could get worse."

"Just give me what I need and I'll be fine," she whispered into his ear. Her tongue dove into the golden convoluted canal again and again while her lips nipped and tugged at his outer ear.

He brusquely pulled her away and kissed her fiercely. She returned the urgent questing of his tongue in full measure, and the insistent heat at the apex of her thighs intensified.

His shirt was off in an instant, her hands already struggling with the snap of his jeans before it even reached the floor. She whimpered in frustration when she discovered his jeans had a button closing instead of a zipper. Her assault had excited him, making the denim pull tautly across the full force of his manhood and hindering her attempts to undo the closing.

Breaking from his kiss, she sank to her knees and embraced his thighs. She rubbed her head against him and kissed the bulging denim, her need for him almost overwhelming her.

"Lin-love, please," he whispered roughly. "I don't

86

want to take advantage of you, but there's only so much a man can stand."

Her head still pressing into him, she nodded. He moaned in response. A moment later he drew her to her feet and led her into her bedroom. "To bed, my Lindsay," he whispered.

She stood near the bed, her gaze locked with his. His rapid breathing told her he read the message there. As his green eyes were held by her blue ones, she carefully, deliberately unbuttoned her blouse and let it slide down her arms to the floor.

But she felt slightly unsteady and dropped her gaze. Quickly ridding herself of the rest of her clothes, she boldly went to him and began to unbutton his jeans. When he stood nude before her, she took a moment to savor the sight of him, the dim glow of evening highlighting rather than obscuring the lines of his body.

Lying on the bed, she watched him lower his body next to hers. "You're beautiful," she murmured, reaching out to touch him. But somehow the urgency that had been driving her had faded, and as she ran her fingers over his chest and firm stomach, it was with a sense of wonder and delight instead of consuming passion.

Kit's need was still evident, and she snuggled close to tease him with her lips and tongue. She lay across him, her head resting on his shoulder, and kissed him.

Returning the sensuous pressure, he apparently didn't notice her kisses becoming less and less insistent.

"Honey, I tried to resist you. I really tri—Lindsay?" he whispered. "Lindsay, are you asleep?"

"Ummm?" She cuddled closer to him and felt him

chuckle ruefully. Fading into a dream, she thought she heard him utter a long drawn out expletive, though she couldn't tell if it was of relief or disappointment.

CHAPTER FIVE

Something woke her. She lifted her head off the pillow and discovered it was three times too big. She also discovered her right leg was comfortably tucked between two masculine ones.

Kit.

Oh, no, did she really do what she thought she'd done? Carefully sliding out of bed, she saw her clothes on the floor next to his jeans and came to the inescapable conclusion that she had. She'd led him on, practically seduced him, and then zonked out at the last minute.

Would he ever forgive her? She knew men had names for women who did that sort of thing, ugly names, but she'd never thought they'd apply to her.

The pounding in her aching head worsened when she stood, but a giant stomach growl gave her a clue as to what had awakened her and she cautiously went to the kitchen. She was ravenously hungry. Some digging around in a cupboard came up with a bag of cookies, and she ripped it open and dug in. Mmmmm, could anything taste so good? Yes, a tiny voice answered, and he's sleeping in your bed.

She was on her ninth or tenth cookie before she realized she hadn't had anything to eat since breakfast. No wonder the cookies were disappearing as fast as quarters into an arcade game.

Twenty minutes later she heard a shuffling sound down the hall that told her Kit was awake and heading for the kitchen. She also noticed two things: she'd eaten half the bag of cookies, and she was stark naked.

Kit entered the room, and she opened a cupboard and threw the remaining cookies inside, resolutely ignoring the ominous sounds that resulted. There wasn't any hope for the second problem, though she looked longingly at the roll of paper towels just out of reach.

"Are you all right, honey?" he asked, peering at her in the dark kitchen. Seeing her only a few feet away, he held out his arms and gave her a sleepy hug. "I was afraid you might be sick after all that stuff you drank."

"No, I'm feeling much better," she said. She'd never known how nice it felt to be naked and be hugged by a man who was naked, too. The lack of ardor both comforted and reassured her. At that moment no barriers existed between them, and she felt strangely content.

He kissed her gently but quickly. "You certainly know how to make a guy feel wanted."

She blushed crimson. "Kit, what I did—I'm sorry. You have every right to hate me forever, I know, but I hope—I hope you won't."

"Hate you?" he said incredulously. "Don't be ridiculous!" He pinched her chin and kissed her briefly. "I do, however, want a rain check."

She blushed again at the unveiled want in his voice.

Stepping back, he said, "I don't want you to worry in the morning. My bike's in the back of your car, and I'm going to ride to my place to work out before opening the shop. I'll stop by your office later on to see how you're doing."

At the reminder of her earlier drunken state, Lindsay stiffened. "You don't have to do that. I feel as good as new." He looked at her skeptically and she amended, "Well, almost as good as new."

"I knew it," he said, smiling. "Now let's go back to bed and get some sleep. Morning comes awfully early for me."

He put his arm around her shoulder and drew her close. Feeling their bare hips pressed together as they walked down the hall, Lindsay felt a rush of unfulfilled desire and brutally crushed it before it could overwhelm her. By the time she lay in his arms again, there was only a vague feeling of being unsatisfied about something. But that, no doubt, would be gone in the morning.

Unfortunately, it didn't work out that way. She only sleepily remembered being kissed good-bye when Kit left in the morning, but by the time she arrived at her office, her memory had improved considerably.

Mortified at what she had done, she walked around the back of the building to avoid being seen through the store windows in Kit's shop, then spent a long day testing her program.

The problem with writing software, though, was that testing it meant sitting around for long stretches of time waiting for a program to assemble or link—

stretches of time she spent plotting revenge against John and thinking of ways to avoid seeing Kit.

Through the windows she could see all the traffic going in and out of his shop. He'd probably be busy all day preparing cyclists for that training ride on Saturday. The training ride! Did he still expect her to go? She had to think of a way to get out of it. What could she do anyway? Change a flat tire?

Balking at the idea of having to confront him, she cowardly decided to play it by ear. She snapped at the rubber band confining her braid in agitation until the memory of Kit unwinding it made her flush with unexpected heat.

Quickly dropping the rope of hair, she figured out that if she went home early and arrived late the next morning, she'd be able to avoid any direct contact with him.

But by Friday afternoon she had to acknowledge that only part of her plan was working. She'd managed not to see him, but avoiding Kit in the tempting flesh had made it harder to deal with her arousing memories of him, and her lack of sleep proved it.

Then even the successful part of her plan failed when Kit showed up on her office doorstep, smiling a greeting.

"Hi, honey. I can't stay long—we're swamped and Rog can only manage for a few minutes," he said, bending to give her a quick kiss as she sat in front of the ten-fifty. "Feeling better?"

"You didn't have to check up on me," she said. Sighing, she sat back in defeat. How could she hope to discourage their relationship when she felt so *glad* to see him? She'd expected to feel embarrassment or chagrin, not the simple contentment that filled her heart.

"I wanted to." He pulled up a chair and sat down next to her. Idly playing with her braid, he snapped the rubber band, and suddenly their eyes met. Azure and viridian met and held, the memory of their night together almost tangible in the air between them.

Softly he added, "I also wanted to call in that rain check."

Startled, Lindsay sat upright. "Rain ch-check?" Oh, God, what could she say?

"You owe me a dinner, remember?" He fanned the tuft of her braid over his face and inhaled the fragrance of her hair. "You, ah, got sidetracked last time," he said with a wicked glint in his eyes, "if you recall."

"I recall," she said in a faint whisper.

Gently releasing her hair, he said, "Seven-thirty okay? There's a great restaurant up in La Jolla I think you'll like."

Remembering what had happened after their last dinner together, Lindsay tried to wriggle out of going. "It looks like it might rain and I'm having trouble getting the top up on my car. Why don't we make it for sometime next week?"

Laughing, he said, "I didn't expect you to drive anyway, honey. I don't bicycle *everywhere,* you know." He stood, reaching out to tuck an errant curl behind her ear. "I'll pick you up—seven-thirty, remember. Right now I've got to get back before Rog panics. See you later."

Ten minutes later her brother stopped by.

"You!" she cried the second he entered her office. "Where's John, the creep? Didn't the coward have enough guts to show himself today?"

Looking surprised—and innocent—her brother said, "What are you talking about? I'm meeting the gang over at that place on Pacific Highway and came by to see if you want to join us."

"You could've phoned." She sounded belligerent, but she half-entertained the ignoble idea of going with her brother instead of Kit.

"Lindsay, I also wanted to see how you were feeling," he said. "I guess John's cure worked."

"Hah!" She suddenly felt very noble.

"What's *that* supposed to mean?"

"His 'cure' could've killed me!" she said, her eyes flashing with outrage. Flushing slightly, she added, "It's a good thing Kit stopped by and took me home, otherwise I'd have been driving home soused to the gills with Margaritas!"

"What? He told me it was his favorite cure—but he didn't say anything about it being a hundred and twenty proof!" Her brother frowned when he realized how much danger she could have been in. "John and I are going to have a nice l-o-n-g talk."

"Thanks, Loge."

"I'm sorry, sis; I had no idea. Are you sure you're all right?"

"My throat's still a little sore, that's all." She gave him a quick hug. "Now go on and have a good time."

The nobility faded when Logan walked out the door, and in a moment of panic she almost called him back. But, cursing her predicament, she locked her office and drove home.

"Oh, Kit, what a marvelous place!" she said, sitting next to him in his VW Scirocco. "That orange and walnut salad was divine."

Heading north on Torrey Pines Road toward Del

Mar, he smiled at her and said, "And now for dessert and a nightcap."

"I don't know where I'll fit it. I really pigged out on that grilled red snapper."

"It won't take up any room at all," he said enigmatically.

Suddenly he slowed and made a U-turn. Parking in an empty roadside lot, he turned to her and smiled. "There. The finest nightcap I know: the Pacific."

He helped her out of the car and guided her down the rough scree, his hands constantly around her waist. Reaching the sand, he gently leaned her against one of the large broken concrete slabs that formed part of the scree and kneeled in front of her.

Her earlier misgivings had dissipated during the delightful dinner, but now a few returned. But all thoughts disappeared when he ran his hand down her left leg from the hem of her black silk skirt to her ankle, where he carefully loosened the strap of her shoe and caressed the bottom of her foot as he removed the black leather sling.

He dealt with her other shoe the same way, making a swell of longing for his touch rush through her.

Carrying her shoes, he held her firmly while they walked along the edge of the wet sand. The nearly full moon turned the surface of the ocean into burnished pewter, giving her the feeling of walking next to a living treasure.

And she felt treasured in the warmth of his arm. "If this glorious place is our nightcap, what's dessert?" she asked dreamily. They walked awhile wrapped in the intimate silence only the constant rumbling of an ocean can provide. Lindsay tried to remember something she'd thought of during dinner, but the sensuous feel of the damp sand through her stockinged feet prevented any too-serious thought from intruding.

Kit stopped near the wild outcropping of stones that marked the beginning of the cliffs. Leaning against a rock with Lindsay held close, he said quietly, "What's dessert? Our time here together."

His kiss was tender, like the lace-edge foam of the Pacific that teased their feet.

"You take a man's breath away tonight, Lin-love," he whispered. His eyes swept over the gold cord woven into her hair and the black and gold silk jacket that hugged her form. "Like a caliph's beautiful daughter, far out of reach."

"But I'm not out of reach, Kit."

"Aren't you?" He sighed and shook his head. "I don't know, Lindsay. Sometimes I think you're more difficult to win than the Tour de France."

"This kind of relationship is new to me," she said, suddenly wanting him to understand. "I'm only used to this kind of intensity in my work. It scares me, Kit. Maybe the ability to have a relationship with anything but a computer doesn't exist for me."

He pulled her into his arms. "Do you remember the folk story of the blue rose? A man searched for years to find what everyone said didn't exist—a blue rose." His kiss on her forehead felt cool in the ocean breeze. "But he found it—and so will I, Lin-love." He tightened his embrace. "All for the love of a caliph's daughter."

Loosening his hold, he lowered his mouth to hers. It started out as a gentle sharing of the night, but soon the kiss deepened with all the power of their unfulfilled passion. Yet Lindsay knew they were both holding back from completely surrendering to that emotion which hovered at the edges of their con-sciences.

She could feel Kit trembling with his restraint as their tongues danced in the ancient steps of longing, trembling against something neither of them had the courage to name.

When they broke from the kiss, his lips sought the soft flesh under the line of her jaw, and her head fell back, welcoming his caress. She slipped her hands beneath his suit jacket and delighted in the warm crispness of his shirt; the boldness that had overtaken her before returned, startling her with its strength.

He strung kisses along the column of her throat, and she began to shake with reaction. His hands stroked her body with loving abandon, the thin silk of her blouse hindering none of his branding touch.

The need that had so overwhelmed her before threatened to burst forth from her control. Her fingers refused to obey her and eagerly unfastened his shirt, diving inside to knead the bare flesh of his muscled frame.

Desire pulled at her like a riptide. She wanted him, and the force of that want terrified her. "No," she whispered aloud in desperation, "no."

His hands and lips stopped their devastation. Holding her shivering body tightly, he comforted her. "What's wrong, Lin-love? Did I hurt you?"

She shook her head. "Kit, I'm frightened. I tried so hard to tell myself not to get involved. But you've been catching me unaware from the first."

Resting her head on his shoulder, he gently rocked her in his arms and she felt safe.

"I thought I could handle it," she said softly, "but Logan was right. This kind of relationship doesn't rely on jump routines and defined equates like a computer program."

"Did you know Logan stopped by to see me this afternoon?" Kit said, his voice a low and calming croon. "He said he wanted to thank me for taking you home the other night." A chuckle went through him. "I didn't tell him you'd amply thanked me yourself."

Logan actually going to talk to Kit? Lindsay pulled away from him slightly to look into his face. "Did he say anything else?"

"It was after I'd closed, so we had a nice long talk." His eyes held her gaze. "Lindsay, he told me about Mara. And why he doesn't think you and I can make a go of it."

She tensed. "What did you answer?"

"The truth. That whatever problems he and Mara had were *their* problems, not ours. And whatever problems *we* have, the ghost of Mara past is not going to be one of them."

Nestling her head on his shoulder once more, she said, "I don't know, Kit. Our worlds are so completely different."

"A man's different from a woman, but I think the differences work out to everyone's satisfaction." He sighed and rested his cheek against her hair. "At least let us try, Lin-love."

She'd been so busy convincing herself their relationship would be a disaster, she hadn't taken the time to think about making it work. Suddenly she remembered what she'd thought of at dinner. Mara and Logan had been *married,* and most of her ex-sister-in-law's depredations had been because of her legal status as a wife.

Maybe she was jumping the gun with Kit and

herself. Maybe . . . "I'll try, Christopher Nathaniel Hawthorne, I'll try."

An exuberant hug answered her.

"It's getting late," he said after a long, peaceful silence. "I'd better take you home. I've got to pick you up at an ungodly hour tomorrow morning."

Gazing deeply into his eyes, she said, "Your home would be fine."

His swift, passionate kiss told Lindsay how much her words meant to him. "Honey, believe me, there's nothing I'd rather do than take you there." He brushed her cheekbone with his lips. "But if I did, I wouldn't be in any condition to ride tomorrow."

"Another rain check?" she teased.

Laughing, he whirled her around and around until they were knee deep in water.

Her legs were suspended in the air as he held her against his body. "Ah, Lin-love, when I call in *my* rain check and you call in *yours*. . ." He let his eyes and lips finish his sentence.

"Your rain check?" she asked when she could breathe again. "I thought you already called it in tonight. Wasn't that what dinner was all about?"

"*That* one was for the dinner you'd promised to have with me. You owe me another one."

Lindsay blushed in confusion at the blatant reminder of her aggression and moved to be released, but sliding down his hard body to the sand didn't help her think any straighter.

"Kit—" she began, but he hushed her with a kiss.

"I won't listen to any regrets about that night. It's every man's fantasy to have a woman want him that much. I came too close to having that fantasy come true to give up now."

She shuddered in fear and anticipation.

CHAPTER SIX

"I don't know why I'm doing this," Lindsay said, climbing into the bike shop van.

The early morning made her vulnerable, and when Kit smiled at her sullen tone, she had to look away. He was dressed in his skin shorts and form-hugging jersey again; that and his smile made her sluggish blood increase its tempo.

"But you *are* doing it," he said cheerfully, "and that's what's important."

To the east the pale pink of dawn limned the distant mountains. It seemed as if only a few hours had passed since she'd fallen asleep. She counted back and realized only a few hours *had* passed.

Groaning, she slumped in the seat and said, "Don't cyclists ever sleep late?"

"Occasionally, but it's a habit most cyclists can't afford," he said. "And I mean that literally. Training usually only fits in in the early morning, before you go to work. It's really the only time you'll have both sun and light traffic."

"Even for an amateur?" she asked with a yawn.

"Actually, that schedule would only work for

amateurs. This is my last year as a pro, so I've been doggin' it a little. The shops are taking more and more of my time, and it's hard to put in the kind of hours the professional circuit demands."

" 'Doggin' it'? You mean you've been taking it *easy*?" With workouts at five-thirty in the morning and hundred-mile training rides? Without thinking she blurted, "I'm glad I didn't meet you when you were putting in really hard hours!"

The statement startled her. She knew it would have been better for both of them if he *hadn't* had time for her, but she'd said the truth: She was glad she could spend some time with him. The thought brought a blush, but Kit only smiled.

Wanting to change the subject quickly, she asked, "Where exactly are we going?" They'd been heading north on Interstate 5 for a half hour or so, but he still gave no sign of turning off the freeway.

"We're riding up El Camino Real, starting south of Cardiff-by-the-Sea, then over to Escondido, down to Rancho Santa Fe and back here. It's all on marked bike routes, so we shouldn't have too much trouble."

"What about me?"

"I was hoping you'd be willing to drive this van as our sagwagon," he said. He gestured to the back of the van, where several bicycles were strapped in along with a large water cooler and ice chest.

She looked at the collection of tools and spare wheels piled behind the driver's seat. "How much mechanical work would I have to do? I'm pretty good with electronics, but gears and chains . . . I don't know. I might need someone to ride with me to handle the tricky stuff."

He laughed with a strange kind of exuberance, reaching out to run the back of his fingers lightly along her cheek. "You're so very special, do you know that?"

Still smiling when he eased the van over to the freeway exit, he said, "We all do our own repairs, honey. You won't have to do a thing but be ready for us at the feeding stations along the way."

He drove into an empty bank parking lot and pulled up next to several other cars. Putting his hand on the door handle but not opening it, he added, "Thanks for being willing to pitch in. It means a lot to me."

Rog came up and opened the door for her before she could respond. "Glad to see Kit convinced you we won't 'byte,'" he said, then waited successfully for her groan at his pun. He indicated the dozen cyclists behind him with a wave, mostly men and women she'd met in Kit's shop. "I think you know everybody, except for maybe Steve Hanson—he works in Kit's College Grove store." Lindsay nodded a greeting.

After listening to instructions on running the sagwagon, she surreptitiously watched the women cyclists out of the corner of her eye. Maybe she should try to tone up a little bit.

One of the women, apparently a veteran, was soothing a newer rider who was complaining of having gained weight after she'd started to ride regularly. Lindsay looked at the sleek young woman and thought she must've been remarkably thin; then she heard the veteran rider explain that muscle weighs more than fat and that the young woman should concern herself with body fat ratios rather than weight.

Would exercise do anything for her? Watching Kit give some last-minute tips about the route to the

102

women, Lindsay decided it was certainly worth thinking about.

Kit walked toward her, his muscles moving seductively under his clothes, and Lindsay had to admit how much he affected her. Licking her suddenly dry lips, she said, "Any last-minute instructions for me?"

Smiling down into her eyes, he shook his head. He tilted her chin up and kissed her lightly. If any of the cyclists had been curious about her status, they suddenly knew where matters stood.

"I'm going to miss you on this ride," Kit said, his voice low. "I like having you beside me."

Ignoring Roger's pleased grin and some of the others' raised eyebrows, she said, "I'll be near you."

He looked like he wanted to say more, but one of the women dropped her helmet and the mood was broken. Giving Lindsay one last kiss, he put on his own helmet and mounted his bike.

Twelve hours later Lindsay drove back into the bank parking lot. The riders were only a few miles behind her and would soon straggle in. At the last pit stop Kit had said it had been a remarkably successful ride, and he'd made her feel part of that success.

He was the first of the riders to return, and she waved to him, holding a cup of cool water for him to drink when he dismounted.

"Thanks," he said, downing the water in one swallow. "My time's pretty good, but I'm glad the route wasn't any longer. I'm getting too old for this."

Lindsay just shook her head and handed him a towel. The other riders started to drift in, all hot and thirsty. When Roger came in, she could see exhaustion dimming his usually sparkling dark eyes, but he rode up to her and Kit with a wide smile.

"Ms. Computer Lady, I wish you would pound some sense into this guy," Roger said, pointing to Kit with his thumb. "All this retirement talk is nonsense. *Nobody* has a kick like Kit Hawthorne!"

"It takes more than a final burst of speed into a sprint to win, Rog," Kit said, affectionately looping a towel around the younger man's neck. "Next year you'll move from the junior to the senior classification, and I don't think I could stand the competition."

When a grinning Roger rode off to the group he'd arrived with, Lindsay instinctively knew Kit didn't want to talk about his own performance and she asked general questions about the ride.

"Can you explain this classification business to me? I've heard some of the others talking about juniors, seniors, veterans, but I'm not sure what it all means."

Stretching his muscles to avoid cramps, Kit smiled at her interest and said, "The United States Cycling Federation tries to make sure people who enter races are qualified, so it licenses amateur racers in classifications: Midgets are the youngest, then it goes to intermediate, junior, senior one and two and then several ranges of veterans, which start at age thirty-five. Next year, when I'm no longer a pro, that's where I'll be ranked."

Still hot from his ride, he dribbled water over his head, then blotted it with the towel.

Aware of his exhaustion, Lindsay said, "Everyone else is almost ready to go. Let's go on home. I'll drive."

"You're a doll."

She drove directly to his house, and once there, Kit headed straight into the shower. Ten minutes later, dressed only in running shorts, he spread out on the living room carpet and began a series of stretching exercises.

She watched his body move in the long, graceful cool-down exercises, his muscles bunching and relaxing in a steady rhythm that her heart soon matched. Tenderness for him welled inside her, and she wished she could somehow soothe away his pain.

Collapsing next to her on the sofa when he'd finished, he said, "That's the one thing I miss on the training rides. Masseurs are always available on the pro circuit, and I could sure use one right now."

"Would an amateur do?" she offered impulsively.

Looking at her intently, he said, "An amateur would do superbly."

He stood and, after throwing a pillow from the sofa onto the carpet, disappeared for a few minutes. When he returned he handed her a bottle of oil and then stretched out again on the floor on his stomach.

"Have you ever given a massage before?" he asked, getting comfortable. When she shook her head, he said, "Don't worry. Just remember a few basics. Rub away from the heart on my arms and legs—you're trying to force blood and energy to flow outward. Work with the weight of your body on your hands." He turned toward her, lifting himself on one arm. "And relax—that's the most important thing."

She kneeled beside him, her knees at his waist. "Does it matter where I start?" she asked, looking at the vast amounts of exposed skin facing her and having second thoughts about her volunteering.

"Not really, though most start up by the shoulders," he said. "It'll be easier if you straddle me."

"Oh." Offering to do this had definitely not been one of her smarter moves. She eyed the bottle of oil skeptically. Was she really supposed to use that, too?

Holding her breath, she put one knee across his narrow hips and reached for the oil. She straddled him carefully, being sure not to touch him with her knees while she poured out the oil. The light green tint surprised her, as did its enticing masculine scent. It was hard to pinpoint it—not musk though not citrusy either—but she found it pleasant all the same.

Her hand tilted to drip the oil onto his back, but she stopped before any could escape.

How would a professional masseuse handle this situation? She'd probably think of him as just a bundle of muscles that needed the kinks worked out, concentrating on first this muscle and then that one.

Lindsay's problems were that she didn't know a deltoid from a trapezius and that the "bundle of muscle" lying on the floor beneath her was the most gorgeous and arousing set of muscles she'd ever encountered. And *that* certainly wasn't a professional attitude.

Letting the oil dribble onto his shoulders, she gritted her teeth and leaned forward to smooth the silky liquid over the tense muscles around his neck. She kneaded the slick golden skin hard, trying to ignore the warmth under her hands.

Her thumbs rubbed the cords of his neck, sinking deep into the hollow at the base of his head. The movements were supposed to help Kit relax, to help the tenseness leave his body, but the motions benefited Lindsay too. As the rigid tension of her body melted away, she unconsciously relaxed against him until her thighs nestled next to his waist.

But while her uneasiness lessened, tendrils of another more powerful emotion began to unwind through her body. Her hands left his neck and traveled down the length of his back, the palms of her hands pressing spirals deep into the tired muscles. The pressure of her hands matched his breathing without her realizing it, making their bodies move in a subtle, elemental rhythm.

The character of her touch changed as that rhythm took hold, twining with the latent unfulfilled desire rising within her. Their bodies became a unified organism, her hands answering the needs of his body without question or hesitation.

"Ummm, perfect," Kit said, stirring beneath her pushing palms, but her concentration remained unbroken. Working downward, she drew her kneading hands over the rise of his buttocks to his thighs. The living sculpture of firm muscle under her hands impelled her to bask in the sensuous touch of hair-roughened legs.

Twice in the past week her body had been driven to a fever pitch without release, and now it took over, giving no warning and leaving only an urgent, insistent desire growing in her loins.

She massaged the woven steel bands of his thighs, her hands reaching higher and higher until her fingers slipped under his running shorts with every upward stroke. There, at the junction of the firm, hard flesh that marked the beginning rise of his buttocks, she let her touch roam inward. Kit moaned in response.

Her active hands descended once more to the solid piers of his legs. When she gently caressed the backs of his knees, she heard his quick intake of breath. On impulse she planted a fleeting kiss on the soft, sensitive skin there. He moved again, but she sat on his ankles and her stern hands prevented him from escaping her touch.

The muscles of his calves fascinated her, and her thumbs furrowed down the middle of them. At his ankles, she kneeled and drew her tongue over the mound of his ankle bone.

In response Kit turned quickly and pulled her to him, his mouth meeting hers in a sudden kiss that stunned them with the strength of its desire. That powerful desire took hold of her, the rough water of her passion hammering against the dam of her control until it cracked, spilling over with all the longing and need and want her body had been denied.

They were both calling in their rain checks.

Lying next to Kit on the floor, Lindsay let their kiss lengthen while her hands roamed his body to create a new kind of tension. The abandon she'd felt the night he'd stayed in her apartment stole over her once more, and one hand caressed the dimple in the small of his back while the other dipped below the elastic waistband of his running shorts.

A moan reverberated from deep inside his chest when her hand settled over the firm mound. Her actions spurred him on. Lightly callused fingertips slid under her blouse and, making quick work of unfastening her bra, gently held the full ripeness of one breast. His thumb went back and forth across the taut rose peak like a metronome marking time with her fevered pulse.

A woman's voice moaned in pure pleasure, and Lindsay didn't immediately recognize that primal sound of feminine satisfaction as her own. She rolled onto her back, and Kit hovered over her while his fingers explored the tiny pale fold behind her ears. Then his hands followed the contours of her neck

108

and shoulders downward to the opening of her blouse, and he quickly discarded that cotton impediment. Her jeans quickly followed.

His hands tenderly kneaded the soft flesh of her breasts while the thumb and forefinger of each hand rolled and pinched the aching nipples. Writhing in pleasure, her body arced upward into his in an unconscious gesture appealing for release.

She felt the heated force of his manhood against her thigh, and a burst of white-hot passion shot through her. The insistent need within her was like the warmth of the noonday sun, making her body temperature rise with all the heat of summer boiling out from that touch.

His hands left her breasts to trace the outline of her waist, while his lips paid tribute to the flat of her stomach and the well of her navel. Stroking the delicate area behind her knees, he kissed and nipped down the top of her thighs, then began the journey upward by sensually sampling her velvety inner thighs.

A cry broke from her when his tongue darted into that moist core of her womanhood. She wanted the fulfillment his tongue promised, but a stronger need overwhelmed her, a need to feed the desire piercing her like laser blasts until it would almost burst of its own accord.

Instead of arching her hips into him, she grasped his shoulders and pulled him up to her. As she kissed him fervently with all the force of her desire, gentle pressure rolled them over until he was lying beneath her. Stroking downward over his hard chest and stomach, her hand quickly found its goal. The full strength of his arousal strained against his running shorts, branding her fingers with its blaze through the thin material. Her face lowered to her caressing fingers.

"Lin," he panted hoarsely, "Lin-love, do you know what . . . Are you sure . . . ?" But his words finished with a groan of masculine pleasure as her lips pressed against the straining contours of his shorts.

She kissed the juncture of his thigh and hip while her hands reached underneath him to the twin mounds of hard flesh.

"I want you, Kit," she murmured against the firm ridges of his stomach. Her lips pulled at the tiny hairs leading from his navel to disappear under the waistband of his shorts, making the exquisite pain of passion roar through her veins like timpani in an orchestra. "I want you so badly I hurt with it."

The shorts were quickly discarded, and for the second time that night, Kit drew Lindsay above him. Kissing her thoroughly, he guided her down to join with his active manhood.

They were both still for a moment, as if on the brink of being overcome. Lindsay had never known she could be filled with such ecstasy, and she could do nothing but string tender kisses all along the perimeter of his face to express her ineffable emotion.

Slowly Kit began to move beneath her, his hips rising to meet hers with metered urgency. Her breasts sensuously crushed against his smooth chest, she drifted in the fog of rapture he was creating with each upward motion and heard only their rough breathing marking the rhythm of their bodies.

Then with a feminine gasp of pleasure-laden surprise, even that sound faded as the taut thread of her passion tightened, drawing her up to the precipice.

The roaring, rushing flood of release burst over the edge, and her cry pierced the night.

A masculine cry was wrenched from Kit before the last waves of her cry had disappeared.

"My Lin-love," he whispered reverently, holding her close. "I never knew life—or my arms—could hold such joy."

Resting contentedly in his embrace, Lindsay kissed the hollow of his shoulder. "Lin-love," she said experimentally. "Why do you call me that?"

His arms tightened. "Lin sounds like yin, and yin, very simply, means the feminine part of the universe in Chinese philosophy." He gently kissed her forehead. "And that's what you are to me—the missing half of my universe. You're everything I ever fantasized a woman could be. Brilliant, beautiful . . ." Lowering his mouth, his lips whispered against hers in a phantom kiss. "And incredibly desirable."

They made love again, and afterward, exhaustion and the sensual lethargy of loving's aftermath assured them of a deep, satisfying sleep in each other's arms.

Morning rapidly arrived, and though Lindsay recalled vague dreams of being carried, her memories of the night before overrode them. Yawning and stretching with languorous abandon, she rolled over to snuggle against Kit.

The surface under her echoed the movement, but she didn't notice. She only noticed that she was in bed alone. The warm greeting hovering inside her shattered, leaving her with a hundred tiny wounds of despair at his desertion of her.

Tilting her head, she detected a faint metal click coming from the floor below. Her head sank to her arms. He was *exercising*! After all they'd shared last night, he'd still rather pump iron than be with her.

She'd always known it would be this way, yet she'd foolishly gone on hoping she and Kit wouldn't be like Mara and Logan—but how else could it be?

No! She would *not* cry! Curling into a ball, she tensed and carefully controlled her breathing to prevent the pinprick tears of despair from spilling down her cheeks. But the pain grew, intensifying with each distant crack of his pounding weights. She covered her ears with her hands, trying to rid herself of that torturous sound, but the steady clicking remained inside her skull.

However much Kit might think of her as a fantasy come true, he always returned to the physical reality of his world—a reality where she had no place.

She had to get away. Silently descending the carpeted stairs to the middle level of his house, she blanked her mind while she gathered her scattered clothes. The clicking was louder here, and she had to leave or go mad from the sound.

After frantically donning her jeans and blouse, she sped from the house, not caring when the door slammed shut behind her in a sudden gust of wind.

She ran the entire six blocks to her condominium, though her knees shook with fatigue as she ascended the steps to her front door. Hot from her run, she only wanted to collapse on the sofa, but being still brought back memories and pain, so she headed for the shower.

The phone began to ring while she was blow-drying her hair, and she froze for a second before quickly switching off the dryer. She went to her desk in the corner of the living room and stared at the phone, letting it ring unanswered.

It was probably Kit, but even if it wasn't, she didn't want to talk to anyone right then. But if she didn't answer, Kit might very well come over. What could she do?

The ringing stopped. A glittering pile of quarters and game tokens next to the phone caught her eye and, scooping them up, she grabbed her purse and headed out the door.

Ten minutes later she parked next to the video-game parlor near her office. Back when she and Logan had developed their first computer, Lindsay had discovered how easily a rowdy video game could defuse anger or frustration. There'd been a lot of both in the early days of TCS, but after a quick game they could return to work with a clear head.

She slid into the seat of the enclosed galactic war game and fed in a dollar's worth of quarters. A few seconds later she was speeding off into interstellar space, zapping alien baddies into cosmic dust.

Surrounded by the sound of explosions and revving starship engines, she was thoroughly absorbed by the game until a hand on her shoulder startled her. She lost a ship when she jumped in surprise.

"Don't you know arcade protocol?" she shouted without taking her eyes off the fast-moving images on the screen. "Put your quarters on that ridge—you'll get to play when I'm done."

"Lindsay," Kit shouted above the noise of the games around him, "we need to talk and we can't do it here."

She risked a glance at his serious face and lost another ship. He had bent over to peer into the tiny interior of the game enclosure she was in, his eyes level with hers.

"What's there to talk about?" she asked. "You like

113

to spend Sunday mornings snuggled up to your bench press; I like to spend them being space captain." Destroying another three alien ships, she added, "Don't let me keep you from your iron maiden."

"Is that why you ran out?" he asked, surprise in his voice. "My morning workouts are just a habit—it was nothing against you." He hit the side of the galactic war game in frustration when Lindsay ignored him, earning a glare from the clerk in the change booth. "This is ridiculous! We've got to talk."

The sound of two alien ships exploding was his only answer.

"Lindsay," he said. There was a warning note in his voice, but she ignored that, too.

He stood with a disgusted sigh, and she felt a moment of painful exhilaration at having won—until first a sneaker-clad foot, then a thigh encased in brief shorts, then the rest of him squeezed into the small booth next to her.

"Kit, stop it! There's not enough room in here for both of us!" she cried. "Kit!"

In a matter of seconds she found herself hunched over on his lap, the game's joystick forgotten.

"*Now* will you listen to me?" he asked, his words partially muffled by her blouse.

"Kit, this is absurd!" His arms tightened around her and she bumped her head trying to squirm away. "Okay, okay, we'll talk—but not here. Let's go to my office."

The scene was becoming a familiar one: she seated on the chair at her desk and Kit on the chair in front of the ten-fifty computer. And just as familiar was the tension inside her.

"How did you find me?" she asked.

"Luck. When you didn't answer your phone at home," he began, then, seeing her guilty start, he added, "for whatever reason, I called your office. Even though you didn't answer, I still thought you might have come down here, so I drove by. I just happened to see your car in the arcade parking lot. I would've called your brother next."

She started to answer, but he held up his hand. "Lin, I'm sorry about this morning," he said, leaning forward to rest his elbows on his knees. "I had no idea it would bother you. I would never intentionally do anything to hurt you."

Frowning, she said slowly, "I know that, Kit. But I also know our relationship—"

"Give us a chance, Lin-love. Granted, this isn't your everyday relationship—but we're not everyday people, either." Kit came over to her and pulled her up to stand before him, his hands gripping her arms. "I always knew I could never settle for an ordinary woman. I don't need an echo of my own way of thinking but someone who will challenge me, make me see the world differently than I'd ever seen it before."

Differently. Why couldn't he see they were *too* different? "But what about the women in your shop, and the ones on the ride yesterday, like Jenny? They know what you mean when you talk about sew-ups or—or gear ratios. They probably work out like you do and eat like you do. Can't you see you'd be happier with someone like them?" Lindsay ignored the catch in her voice, and in her heart.

Smiling ruefully, Kit kissed her forehead. "You make it sound as if I should fall in love with a female version of my clone."

"No, no, that's not what I meant," she said, confused because it *had* sounded like that.

"Honey, you said you'd try to make it work between us," Kit said. "That includes letting me know when something I do bothers you." His arms went around her, pulling her close. "You can't imagine what I felt when I discovered you gone this morning. Suddenly half my world was empty."

She felt him laugh softly. "There're tire tracks halfway down my street, I left so fast."

"I shouldn't have left this morning," she said. "I'm sorry. I just panicked. You may have noticed I'm not at my rational best in the morning."

"Sometimes you're at your best when you're not so rational," he said, an intimate smile warming her as he stroked her hair.

She would try to make it work between them; make it work without losing hold of that cool rationality she depended upon. But that thought was mocked by the warmth his smile kindled inside her, and she suddenly knew her heart's commitment had already been made.

CHAPTER SEVEN

After staying up half the night thinking of her relationship with Kit, Lindsay overslept and barely made it to the eight o'clock meeting she and her brother had scheduled with the new chief executive officer at Trent Computer Systems. It went well. The woman they had chosen was doing an excellent job of getting TCS back on track, and two hours later Lindsay drove to her office feeling better about the company than she had since Mara had shown up.

Smiling at a bicyclist she recognized who rode past when she slowed for a car ahead, she recalled the CEO's words. "Now all we have to do is hear from the lawyers that the litigation has been successfully concluded and TCS can really move ahead."

It was a time to look forward and plan a future for more than just a computer company.

A few blocks from her office a GRAND OPENING sign caught her eye while she waited at a stoplight. A fitness center was offering a special price on an aerobics dance class, and Lindsay impulsively turned in to the parking lot.

Climbing the stairs to her office, she shook her

head at signing up for three classes a week starting at nine each morning. Did she really think she could do it? Did she really think she could compete with . . .

"Oh, Kit," she whispered to the empty air. A haphazard bouquet of wildflowers was tucked into the last fading corner of shadow on the mat outside her office door. A note peeked out of the damp paper towel wrapped around the stems.

> Saw these on my morning ride and missed you all the more, Lin-love. Be with me tonight.
>
> Kit

Lindsay carried the bouquet to the sink and carefully unwrapped the paper towel. A search of her office didn't turn up anything suitable to put the flowers in, so she was reduced to dumping out the contents of her large paper clip box and filling it with water. She smiled dreamily when she propped the note against the makeshift vase on her desk.

Their relationship had grown beyond anything that could be called casual. Instead of a gradual lessening of the initial attraction between them, as she'd expected, it seemed that attraction had intensified logarithmically.

The optimism she'd felt at the TCS meeting still held her—as long as she didn't think about the past or, for now, any further into the future than the night she would spend in his arms.

The next morning she'd just changed into her street clothes after her first exercise class when Kit returned from visiting his El Cajon store.

Embracing her in a quick hug, he said, "Good morning, honey." He tilted her chin up and kissed her soundly. "Do you know how absolutely beautiful you look in the morning?"

"You're not so bad yourself, you know," she said with a warm smile. "But unless you can think of a way to put a computer keyboard on a pair of handlebars, we'd better get back to work."

"Actually I'm here in an official business capacity." He nuzzled her neck and pulled at the tiny hairs escaping her braid with his lips.

Laughing, she said, "I can tell." She gently disengaged herself from his grasp, though the memory of the night of pleasure those same hands had given her urged her to stay in his embrace.

"No, really." Walking to her desk, he flipped through a program listing. "Just how hard is it to program? Think I could do it?"

"Probably," she answered slowly, not sure of his reasons but secretly pleased at his interest. "If you put your mind to it. The frustrating part is realizing how literal a computer is. It will do exactly what you *tell* it to do, not what you *want* it to do."

Searching through her library for an introductory book on programming, she added, "What kind of program were you planning on writing?"

"The biggest problem I have is inventory. I waited three months—and paid a premium price—for a special-ordered part that I just discovered tucked away in a corner out in my El Cajon store. I need to keep much closer tabs on all the parts we get in."

"It'd probably be easier for me to just set up a TrentCalc—"

"Don't you think I could do it?" he interrupted with a touch of defensiveness in his voice that made her realize the inventory program was partly an excuse to better understand her world.

"Of course you could do it, Kit," she said quickly. "It's only that I didn't want you to go through a lot of trouble if you didn't have to."

"It's no trouble."

"Okay. Here are a couple of books on BASIC to get you started. When you think you're ready, I can let you run a program on my ten-fifty." She started flipping through the disk file. "I have a copy of our BASIC here somewhere."

Kit laughed. "Let me guess—it's called TrentBasic, right?"

"What else?" she said, grinning.

Lindsay worked late that evening and didn't see Kit again until early the next afternoon, when he bounded into her office proclaiming complete mastery of programming.

"I've got it!" he said, waving a stack of handwritten notes. "I wrote everything out last night. Now all I have to do is run it."

"Now all you have to do is type it in," she corrected.

She introduced him to TCS's word-processing program and sat back to watch him type in the lengthy piece of computer code. He'd written three programs, two short ones and a longer one. Fighting the temptation to lean forward and scan his program for errors, she tried to work on her own program instead.

She realized having someone peering over your shoulder telling you what to do wasn't the way to learn how to program, but it was hard letting him make the mistakes she could see he was making. So when Logan showed up, she felt relief at the diversion.

Bracing herself for Logan's reaction at seeing Kit seated in front of one of her computers, she was surprised at his mild shrug. "Got some good news," he told her. "Why don't you walk me to my car."

She gave Kit a few instructions on how to run his first short program and then followed Logan down the stairs. At the bottom her brother spun around and, smiling widely, squeezed her in a bear hug.

"It's over, Lin! Mara's attorney telephoned late this morning to say they are withdrawing their last appeal. Trent's still ours!"

Laughing and crying at the same time, Lindsay found herself enveloped in another bear hug. "It's finally over," Logan whispered fiercely.

"Now we can look forward again!" she said, wiping away the tears streaming down her face. A faint noise began coming from her office, but she ignored it while giving Logan another hug. Then she dimly heard Kit calling her over the noise.

"Just a minute, Kit," she cried. "Oh, Logan! I feel as if I can breathe again! When can we start that—"

"Lindsay!" she heard Kit shout, a definite note of panic in his voice.

"Listen, kid, I'd better get back and tell everyone the good news," Logan said, heading for his car. "But I had to tell you in person. Let's celebrate tonight!"

"You got it!" she called before dashing up the stairs to her office. The noise hadn't lessened, and it was beginning to sound ominous.

"Kit, what—" she shouted over the noise, then saw what was wrong. "Oh, no!"

Ribbons of paper spilled in all directions over the

computers and were crawling along the floor in giant loops while the printer kept spewing out more at the speed of a page a second.

"I can't get it to stop," Kit yelled, frantically pushing keys on the keyboard.

Rushing to the computer through the mass of paper, Lindsay popped the disks out and shut the system down. Silence ensued.

Several seconds of quiet passed before Kit whispered, "What happened?"

A chuckle began deep in her throat and quickly grew to a full-blown laugh. She laughed so hard hiccups started, interrupting her explanation.

"I think," she managed to get out before a hiccup caught her, "I think you coded a form feed in a closed loop. Sometimes—" Another hiccup. "Sometimes there's no way out but to shut the system down."

Subdued, Kit moved an armful of computer paper and sank into a chair. "But it *seemed* so easy."

"So does riding a bike," she answered and then hiccuped. "Being able to balance on two wheels doesn't mean I'm ready for the Tour de France."

Grinning at her, he said, "Point taken." His grin widened when she hiccuped again. "Try holding your breath, especially putting pressure on your diaphragm muscle, here." He stood and slid his hand under her blouse, caressing the skin just below her ribs.

She tried it, and they both silently waited to see if she would succeed. No hiccups shook her body, but the slow circles his hand was making generated a reaction all its own.

Their eyes met and held, extending the silence until his mouth descended to hers. It sent the warm brandy of desire surging through her as his kisses always did, but there was a subtle difference, too. Something had been altered between them; an acceptance of their roles that, for Lindsay, gave their relationship a new, more lasting quality that threatened her precarious equilibrium. They were entering a new phase, and she wasn't at all sure she was ready for it.

But she quickly clamped down such thoughts. Breaking from his kiss, she said, "I think my hiccups went away."

"Of course. You can always rely on the famous Hawthorne cure."

"Is that anything like the famous Hawthorne specialty?"

Nuzzling the tender area below her ear, he said, "It *is* the famous Hawthorne specialty."

Lindsay conscientiously attended her aerobics class, but by Friday the stringent exercises caught up with her.

"I thought this was supposed to make me feel better," she muttered to herself as she staggered up the stairs to her office. God, she hurt! She hadn't even had enough energy to change out of her leotards and tights or take a shower.

Collapsing on the futon in the corner, she was completely immobile. Even her leg warmers hurt.

"Hi, honey," Kit said, walking into the office looking healthy and fit. "I need to ask you a question about that TrentCalc. . . . Are you all right?"

She could only groan at his disgusting exuberance.

"Lin, you look exhausted." His eyes narrowed. "What have you been doing?"

"I have spent the past hour in the twentieth century's answer to a medieval torture chamber," she said, shifting slightly and grimacing at the resulting pain. "Did you know dungeons now have mirrors along one wall? And they now charge a hundred dollars for privileges you used to enjoy only if you committed high treason."

Kit gave a shout of laughter. "Have you really been going to an exercise class? Poor Lin-love." He bent in front of the futon and, gently raising her legs, sat in the corner.

Stripping off her leg warmers, he said, "You should have taken a hot shower afterward. You would have felt much better."

"Take a good look at at the insidious design of this thing," she said, snapping the rounded neckline of her leotard. "It was not made for rapid ingress or egress."

"Believe me, I'm looking," he said, massaging the tender calves of her legs.

At any other time his words would have brought a faint tint of pink to her face, but she only moaned her pleasure at his hands relieving the pain in her legs. She drifted along on the tide of his soothing, stroking fingers, the agony flowing out at his touch.

"What you need is a bout with my whirlpool," he said. "Then later this weekend, if you're feeling better, I'll show you that exercise can be fun, too."

"I'd love to vegetate in your hot tub, Kit, but I've got way too much to do." Swinging her legs down, she sat up with a groan. "*After* I take some aspirin."

"Okay," he said, giving her a quick kiss and walking toward the door. "But I'll stop in this afternoon to see if you've changed your mind. That warm, bubbling water feels awfully good to sore muscles."

"Kit, you don't have to treat me like an invalid," she said, laughing at the elaborate tray of food and wine he set down on the dark blue tiles next to his whirlpool. The warm, turbulent water had made all her muscles relax. She even forgot to feel self-conscious about the less-than-adequate two-piece bathing suit she was wearing, and she felt better than she had in months.

Throwing a nearby towel over his arm, Kit said with a grin, "All part of the service, ma'am." He picked up a tiny speared hors d'oeuvre that looked like a meatball and dipped it in a creamy sauce. "May I tempt madam's palate with an exotic treat from the East?"

The sight of him playing the role of a proper waiter while dressed in a pair of astonishingly brief swim trunks brought a smile to her face. Falling into the spirit of fun, she said with an air of mock hauteur, "I'd love to, but I make it a practice never to eat anything I can't pronounce."

"In that case," he said, plopping the hors d'oeuvre back into the sauce bowl, "let me introduce myself. C. N. Hawthorne, language instructor extraordinaire, at your service." Kit quickly slid down next to her in the swirling water.

"Lesson number one. That meatball-looking stuff is called *falafel.*" He held her face in his hands, his thumbs resting in the sensitive furrow between her bottom lip and her chin. "Repeat after me. Fah . . ."

"Fah," she said while his thumbs caressed her lower lip as she tucked it in to pronounce the syllable.

"Lah . . ."

"Lah."

"Ful," he finished, his voice taking on a rougher quality as he watched her mouth form the sounds.

It was hard to tell if the heat she felt came from the water or him, but she instinctively leaned toward him.

"Ful," she said in a whisper.

Clearing his throat, he reached for the toothpick piercing the ball of falafel. "Excellent. Now you can try it."

"Uh-huh," she said. The roiling of the water matched her increasingly unruly pulse, and that, together with his closeness, made her reckless. "What's that tan stuff all over it?"

Seeing her game, he suppressed a smile and said, "Tahini, you wench, tahini." His fingers held it close to her mouth. "Now take a bite."

With a wicked gleam in her eyes, she leaned forward, the edges of her white teeth just visible between her lips. Widening her mouth, her teeth reached out and gently sank into his finger's golden flesh.

She heard his quick intake of breath and it spurred her on. Her hand, dripping water, plucked the toothpick from his grasp and tossed it toward the tray. Immediately her teeth relaxed into a kiss.

Wanting to taste him instead of the spicy dish he offered, Lindsay's lips nipped a path down his index finger, across his knuckles and around to the flesh of his palm. The rasping tempo of his breathing increased when she gently kissed the inside of his wrist.

Each kiss threw tinder onto the fire burning at the very seat of her womanhood; the tinder caught and blazed into long, licking flames of urgent need that were almost physical in their impact. Her tongue traced the path of the prominent vein winding up his arm and discovered that the path led directly to her own inferno.

"Lin-love," Kit moaned, "Lin, what about your sore muscles?"

"Oh, I still ache, Christopher Nathaniel," she whispered, "but it's an ache with a very specific remedy." Her lips followed the ridge of one shoulder while her fingertips danced along the other.

He groaned with that deep-seated passion she knew so well and reached for her shoulders to pull her to him. But she stopped him, leaning away.

"No," she said, dribbling water down his chest. "This time you're calling in your rain check, whether you know it or not."

Late that afternoon something had stirred within her—an emotion she was still too afraid to name. She'd been thinking of Kit's extremely brief programming career and his good-natured acceptance of its demise when she realized that she liked just being around him. He took himself and his work seriously, but he also knew when to laugh.

And when to love.

Lindsay had him lean back against the edge of the hot tub, and his compliance conveyed his tacit acceptance. With the water buoying him, she let her hands slide down his body, past his narrow hips and taut thighs, down to his feet. The water boiled around her while she released one leg and grasped the other one.

Clean, rosy-pink skin lined the bottom of his foot and edged around his toes. She drew it to her mouth, her tongue playing along the ridge below his toes. But the rumble in his chest—almost a purr—quickly crescendoed to a moan of surprise and passion caught unaware when she slipped his little toe into her mouth and sucked gently.

Her relentless mouth moved on to the next toe and the next, each time swirling her tongue around it as she drew it into the hidden recesses behind her teeth.

"Oh, God, Lin," he cried hoarsely, throwing his head back and his chest heaving with his attempts to control his breathing.

He reached down to adjust his swim trunks, no doubt attempting to lessen the painful stretch of material across his turgid manhood, but swiftly coming to his side, she impatiently removed the garment altogether.

"You're too far away," he murmured. "Come closer."

Locking gazes with him, she let the water carry her over his submerged hips and rested her knees on either side of him on the wide, sloping bench that circled the whirlpool. In one continuous motion his hands reached behind her and untied the strings of her bathing suit while he pulled her closer to him.

Their lips met in an explosive kiss. The natural force of that passion rocked her to the depths of her being and sent fiery brands arcing through her body, leaving a trail of sparks like miniature suns to singe her unprotected heart.

The rest of her swimsuit joined his. His hands, too long inactive, roamed insatiably over her. Cupping her breasts, he laced kisses along the upper curve of those pillow-soft mounds until her own head fell back with a moan. His mouth followed the curve of her breasts, then made its way to the peaks.

Replaying the sensuous melody she'd played on his toes, his tongue and gentle teeth ignited every last reserve of desire and need, making her writhe for fulfillment. The water reinforced the roiling of her agitated pulse, and her body reacted with the elemental rhythm of her womanhood.

Kit's hands grasped her hips, and she felt his undiluted virile heat press into the soft folds of her feminine core, merging with the enveloping fire of her own passion.

Their bodies, light and buoyant in the steaming water, moved in an intricate pattern choreographed by the sensuously pummeling jets. Lost to space and time, they had entered that ethereal realm of the senses.

Within Lindsay the fire had grown and intensified until she'd been engulfed in an internal sun. But deeper inside the mass of bright heat suffusing her was another, brighter pinpoint of light. It pulsed each time Kit's and her body met. The tempo of their thrusts increased, and that pinpoint of light grew and grew until it, too, threatened to engulf her.

But just as she felt herself becoming forever lost, the spheres of fire and flame burst in a nova of release and a cry of utter fulfillment was wrenched from her lungs. Kit's own release followed, before the echoes of her pleasure even had a chance to vanish.

She collapsed in his arms, and neither of them moved as the remnants of the fireballs spun along every nerve ending in their bodies.

He kissed her softly. "You leave me breathless, Lin-love," he said, cradling her next to his side. "Being with you is like riding down a mountain—exhilarating, exciting, and leaving me forever on the edge of losing control."

Filled with a delicious languor after their lovemaking, Lindsay only snuggled closer in answer. She could feel his contented rumbling chuckle as he reached for one of the glasses of wine behind them.

"Thirsty?" he asked.

"Ummm," she assented. She took a sip and handed it back to him, warming at his intimate smile when he turned the glass to drink from the place where her lips had been.

After taking another sip from the proffered glass, she said, "I haven't ridden a bike in years. When I was little, though, I was really hot stuff."

She closed her eyes and leaned back into the memory. "One Christmas Logan and I got matching bikes known as English three-speeds, and from then on nobody could catch us. We were horrid to those poor things! Dirt roads, the hill behind our house, even the shallow creek a few blocks away—nothing stopped us."

The long, dark rope of her hair floated in front of him, and he grasped it and idly began to pull off the rubber band. "What about now? I could fix you up with any bike you wanted."

Smiling, she shook her head. "Thanks, but bikes—and cycling—are out of my league now. When you make a mistake in programming all you get is an error message—"

"Or a roomful of paper," he said with a grin.

She laughed. "Or a roomful of paper. But make a mistake in riding and whammo! You get everything from scraped knees to a broken head." Stretching, she added, "And I've had enough pain for a while."

Instead of looking disappointed, as she'd expected, his gaze held a hint of speculation. "Dirt roads and shallow creeks, huh? I'll keep that in mind all the same."

"Kit, that was a long time ago. You know how crazy kids can be!"

"Uh-huh," he said.

He looked a little too innocent. "You're not planning anything, are you?" she asked.

"Me? Nonsense," he said cooly. "More wine?"

When she didn't immediately take the glass he held out to her, he lowered it to the surface of the water and used its round crystal base to trace the small white crescents of the tops of her breasts that were all that showed above the water.

"How are your sore muscles doing?" he asked, his voice almost a whisper.

"They're not sore at all," she said, breathless at the intimate atmosphere. "Thanks to the Hawthorne cure. Again."

Without taking his eyes off her, he quickly put the wineglass on the edge of the hot tub. His light feather touch along her jaw sent a ripple of tension down her spine, and she licked her lips. Kit's hand fell to her shoulder and gently lifted the dark, wet braid draped there. Sliding his hand down to its end under the water, he began to unravel the intricate plait, letting the swirling water separate the strands.

Shivering again, Lindsay murmured, "Though sometimes I think that cure should only be available by prescription."

He said nothing, his intent gaze resting on the fan of midnight satin spreading out before him. Slipping behind her, he ran his hands down her arms to her fingertips.

"Such glory as I have never seen," he said, his mouth tasting the edge of her ear. She leaned back into him but felt him tense when his hands gripped hers.

131

"We've been in here too long," he said, drifting away and climbing out of the whirlpool. Oblivious to the water dripping off his naked body onto the tiles, he reached down and lifted her out of the tub.

He stood close to her and chafed the dimpled skin of her hands. "Why didn't you tell me you were getting waterlogged?"

"It felt so good in there, I didn't notice," she answered, shivering in earnest in the cool evening air.

Grabbing a large towel, he wrapped her tenderly, then haphazardly dried himself. "Let's get some sleep."

Held tightly to his side, she walked up the stairs to his bedroom. Once snuggled next to him in the massive water bed, she could feel the moist heat from the hot tub radiating from his body. Cuddling closer, she couldn't resist asking, "Was that an example of how much fun exercise can be?"

He laughed and kissed her forehead. "No, honey, that's *not* what I was referring to. You'll see on Sunday."

"Sunday? Why not tomorrow?"

"You need another day of recovery."

She giggled. "Does that mean more doses of the Hawthorne cure?"

"Incorrigible," he said tenderly.

The following day, after a long leisurely swim in his pool, she was summarily summoned to his kitchen to be inducted into the mysteries of making homemade pasta. He pulled up a stool for her to sit on so she wouldn't strain her legs and then hovered close as he watched her pile the flour into the middle of a cutting board.

"Excellent," he said in his best professorial voice.

"Now make a well in it and add the eggs." His hand grasped her hand, which held the fork, and he showed her how to carefully stir the eggs into the flour, all the while letting his lips nibble on her ear.

When the doughy mass could no longer be stirred, he reached around from both sides of her and instructed her in the proper pasta dough-kneading technique. His body pressed into hers each time he leaned into the push stroke of the kneading, and she quickly began to lose interest in making pasta.

By the time he'd explained how the pasta machine worked and had cranked through several batches, she could hardly concentrate on the delicate beige strands of fresh pasta she draped over the drying rack.

He so easily overwhelmed her. It frightened Lindsay, and vague threads of fear began to mix with the desire his very presence called into being.

Later on, while the pasta dried in kitchen, Kit pulled out the programming books she'd lent him, and a list of questions. He lounged back on the sofa and motioned for her to snuggle in beside him.

"Rest here, honey," he said. "That's it—put your head on my shoulder. And if you get too tired of answering my questions, just let me know. Okay?"

One of his hands held the paper with questions on it while the other moved in slow, comforting circles over her back. Her eyes were level with his hand that held the paper, but her gaze was focused at some point beyond as she answered his questions as clearly as she could.

After a while her answers started coming slower and slower until they stopped coming at all. Vulnerable in her state of near-sleep, Lindsay felt an emotion she'd long ago suppressed begin to nudge at the confining walls of her heart.

It was an emotion she couldn't bear to acknowledge; an emotion she equated with pain and loss and torment; an emotion that would shake her life to its foundations.

And a ripple of apprehension passed through her when in that one bright lucid moment before sleep claimed her, she realized that the nature and power of her feelings meant that once she acknowledged that emotion—gave it its proper name—she would never be free of it again.

Deep within her a voice ignored the careful rationalizations of her mind.

She loved him. She loved Kit Hawthorne. And she always would.

But there was no panic at the naming of the feeling bursting from her heart, because by then she only dreamed.

CHAPTER EIGHT

"Are you sure this is supposed to be fun?" she asked, standing up very carefully. She hadn't been on roller skates since she'd been a kid, and then it had only been the kind she slid her sneakers into and tightened with a big bulky key. She'd never worn anything like the fancy, urethane-wheeled fastback models on her feet at the moment.

"Sit back down. You're not done yet," Kit said, letting her grab onto him to keep from falling.

"Not done? They're both laced right," she said while she glanced at each skate.

"I wasn't talking about the lacing, honey." Kit disappeared into the tiny roller skate rental shop only a few feet from the ocean in Pacific Beach.

She thought longingly of her office and the nice stable computers just a few blocks away, but Kit reappeared before her thoughts could go any further.

Dumping a pile of molded plastic and Velcroed elastic onto the bench beside her, he said, "Here we go. Knee pads, elbow pads and helmets."

"You're kidding, right?" she said, eyeing the pile warily. "I can't wear all that stuff! I'll look ridiculous."

Ignoring her protests, he pulled a knee pad out of the pile and began strapping it onto her. "Then think how ridiculous you'll look with a cast up to your shoulder instead." She let him finish without another word.

"Okay, we're all set. Let's go," he said, pulling Lindsay to her feet.

"I almost think I'd prefer the torture chamber," she said, taking experimental steps. She wobbled precariously and immediately felt his steady grip on her elbows.

"Relax—it'll all come back to you. You'll do fine. And I'll be here to catch you if you look like you're going to fall."

"Thanks. I think."

Ten minutes later they were sailing down the concrete walk bordering the beach. For over an hour they dodged teenagers who had enormous radios perched on their shoulders, and enjoyed the crisp salt air. She discovered it was hard to watch the colorful crowd and where she was going at the same time, but Kit steered her out of trouble.

"How about an ice cream cone from that shop up ahead?" he asked, holding her hand and skating off toward the store.

Laughing, she let herself be pulled along to the doorway, but as she neared it and tilted her foot forward to drag the toe stop along the sidewalk, she suddenly felt apprehensive. She halted on the threshold, reluctant to go in.

What was wrong with her? It was a perfectly normal ice cream parlor.

"Something wrong, honey?" Kit asked.

There was nothing she could say that wouldn't

sound completely crazy. She brutally crushed her irrational fears and answered him calmly.

"I was only wondering if we're allowed to wear skates inside."

"They would be hard pressed for business if they didn't allow it," he said, leading her to one of the tiny wrought iron tables near the window facing the ocean. "How're you doing? Not too tired?"

When she shook her head, he offered to step up to the counter and place their order. "What would you like? They've got everything from single dips to giant banana splits."

"I'd like a strawberry ice cream soda if they have it," she answered. "There's nothing finer than a really superb soda."

"One superb ice cream soda coming up," he said with a smile.

Lindsay watched him skate up to the clerk and order two strawberry ice cream sodas, the working of the muscles in his strong legs and thighs drawing her eyes. How many men could look sexy in knee pads, elbow pads and a helmet?

With a sudden rush the fear she'd felt at the entrance to the ice cream shop returned. Trembling with the effort to control it, she concentrated on Kit leaning against the glass counter as he watched the clerk filling their order.

He stretched his hands in a gesture she'd seen him make often, especially when he was coming in from a long ride, and she smiled at the intimacy implied in knowing that special movement. But her smile froze when without warning the source of her fear and apprehension overwhelmed her like a wave catching a swimmer unaware.

She loved him! She'd dismissed the uneasy feeling

from her dream the day before, but now she couldn't deny it.

Stunned at her heart's betrayal, she stared at the tabletop with a stricken expression, trying desperately to master the panic simmering so near the surface.

Kit set the two ice cream sodas onto the table and sat down, saying, "You *are* tired! Damn it, I knew we shouldn't have come this far." Sliding her soda toward her, he added, "Drink this. We'll rest here for a while, and then if you don't feel up to tackling skating back, I'll come get you in the van. How's that?"

"No, I'll be fine, Kit," she mumbled, knowing she was lying. "Really."

Most of the fun had left the outing by the time they returned to the skate rental shop. He'd read her mood, so when Lindsay asked to be dropped off at her condo, Kit acquiesced with the simple demand that she take care of herself.

She entered her living room and immediately tripped over a stack of computer magazines she'd set near the door to take to her brother.

"Great," she muttered sarcastically, kicking the tumbling pile out of the way. She threw herself onto the sofa and ignored another stack that went sliding off the end.

"Just great, Lindsay Trent," she said bitterly to the otherwise empty room. "TCS gets saved at the last minute from the hands of a birdbrained gold-digging cat and you're already tossing it back into the ring to get mauled again. Clever. Very clever."

At the moment she had to admit to herself that she felt like a very chagrined moth who, warned about flying too close to a flame, now had to hobble around with singed wings. But just as a moth dances an elaborate waltz with death as its partner in spite of caution, Lindsay had known that each additional day spent with Kit was like another swooping flight through fire.

She'd been a complete fool, thinking she could escape where Logan had been caught. Oh, no! Lindsay would never be so careless. It had been easy to convince herself that she could control her relationship with Kit; easy to convince herself that they could be friends—and lovers—without further commitment. But how could she have been so blind to the "love" in "lovers"?

There was only one solution to the mess she found herself in, but did she have the courage to carry it through?

She was being a coward, and she hated herself for it. Days had passed without her saying anything to Kit, though she'd had the feeble excuse that he'd been visiting his other stores and therefore she hadn't had the chance to say anything really serious.

After a week of assuring Kit she'd recovered and had learned not to press herself to go on in her aerobics class when her body told her to stop, she finally worked up her courage to tell him their relationship needed to cool down for a while.

She picked a time when she knew his shop would have few customers, but still her steps were slow as she descended the stairs. And she couldn't prevent her eyes from taking a quick sad look at the poster that had started everything so long ago.

"Lin, hi!" Kit said cheerfully from behind the counter.

Her eyes remaining on the poster, Lindsay glumly wondered how much longer that cheerfulness would last. His smile hadn't lost the power to make her knees weak or her breath short, and she felt a sharp twinge of pain when she realized she would probably never see it again.

She lowered her eyes from the poster and took a deep breath to give herself courage. But something caught her eye, and her precarious courage effortlessly metamorphosed into curiosity.

It was a new kind of bike, totally unlike the aristocratic ten-speeds Kit normally sold. Though it did have a certain elegance to its lines, it looked more sturdy than sleek, and Lindsay experienced a sudden, inexplicable affinity for it.

Feeling Kit's hands on her shoulders, she moved forward out of his grasp toward the bike. She couldn't afford to come under his spell again, but she felt only relief when he mistook her action for interest. Then she realized with a jolt that he wasn't entirely mistaken—she did like the bike.

"Like it?" he asked. "It's called a Stumpjumper."

An odd, excited note in his voice made her glance at him. She regretted the action immediately when she saw his heart-stopping smile and a mischievous glint in his eyes.

"I do like it," she admitted slowly. "It's not nearly as intimidating as your other bikes."

"Or as temperamental," he said. "In fact, it's perfect for riding on dirt roads and up hills and through shallow streams."

As the implication behind his words sank in, pangs of guilt and uncertainty attacked her. Had he really ordered the bike specially for her? His smile told her he had, and she began to stumble over words to express her surprise.

His voice cut through her gibberish. "There's a race coming up for these kinds of bikes next weekend. It's sort of a mix of cyclo-cross and a 'clunker' race—you're welcome to come watch me."

Lindsay looked at him sharply. Had there been a subtle, challenging emphasis on the word "watch"?

"Clunker? You mean like old bikes? I didn't realize that kind of riding was part of a pro cyclist's circuit," she said, an idea starting to germinate in the depths of her mind.

"It isn't. This race is strictly for fun."

"So there'll be a lot of amateurs?"

"Plenty."

"Can anyone sign up?"

"Anyone."

"When did you say this race was?" This was craziness! Her questions were the product of an enfeebled mind.

"Next weekend," he said, the same hint of challenge in his voice.

"And where?"

"Out by Cuyamaca."

Cuyamaca was a beautiful area up in the mountains, but wild. It was insane even to think about riding in a race there.

"Do you have to sign up in advance?"

His smile looked suspiciously victorious. "You do, but I have the forms in my office." After a long silence he added, "Why?"

Wait—there's only one bike. You're saved! She studied the knobbly tires and stubby handlebars jutting straight out instead of curving downward as they did on regular ten-speeds.

"It looks a little small for you," she said, a tinge of relief shading her words.

"Oh, this one's not for me," he said with all the glee of a jailer telling his prisoner there's no escape. "Mine's back there. I was working on it when you came in."

Realizing she was good and fairly caught, her tension broke and Lindsay started laughing. "Okay, you beast. Where do I sign?"

Grinning at her capitulation, he escorted her back to his office and reluctantly left the door open, since Rog wasn't in the shop that day. But having the door open didn't stop him from giving her a swift hard kiss.

She responded unthinkingly, her lips molding to his without hesitation. Their piercing tongues broke through token barriers and wove an enveloping web of passion with strands of fire.

When he pulled away, she was left feeling confused and ashamed of her body's reactions. How could she hope to convince him their relationship needed to cool for a while when a simple kiss made her melt in his arms?

He leaned against the edge of his desk, where he could watch her and also keep an eye on his shop.

"Fill out these forms and I'll send them in with mine," he said, handing her a thick envelope. "Then I'll give you a couple of lessons tomorrow to get you acquainted with the bike. In this kind of race you need to grab for the brakes without having to think about where they are."

She moved toward the door to return to her office, her courage having completely deserted her. "Er, thanks. See you tomorrow then."

"Oh, Lindsay," he said, halting her flight. "You

142

looked like you had something on your mind when you came in. Anything important?"

After a long half-minute of silence, her answer was barely above a whisper. "No. No, it wasn't important."

She dreamed of him that night. It began with them cycling side by side through an indistinct landscape. She glimpsed trees and vague hills, but her attention was focused on Kit riding next to her. Looking down, she watched his legs move up and down with each pedal stroke, and the action mesmerized her.

Her eyes followed the hypnotizing up, down, up, down movements until, in the disconcerting way of dreams, he was no longer cycling but jogging. Disturbed by the change, she shifted restlessly in her sleep. Who was that jogging up ahead?

The woman turned, gesturing for Kit to speed up and join her. Mara! She laughed at Lindsay and waved; then her outstretched hand pointed to a distant building where men were gathered with trucks and ladders. Kit was jogging beside Mara now, and they were both laughing at Lindsay while gleefully pointing to the ghostly building.

They jogged inside, and Lindsay started to follow them, but a guard stopped her at the door. She struggled to be let in, but he just held her. Finally the guard began laughing, too, and forced her to look up.

The workmen were lowering a sign that said Trent Computer Systems and replacing it with one saying Hawthorne Computer Systems!

"No! Stop! I won't let you," she cried, waking herself up. It took her several moments to get untangled from the bunched-up sheet holding her prisoner, and when she did, she was flushed and hot. The images of the dream faded slowly, as dreams will, but it left her shaken and uneasy.

Had her dream been a warning, or was it only her overactive imagination? Unsteadily getting to her feet, she went to the kitchen for a drink of water. There moonlight spilled onto the white countertops and made them glow with an eldritch light.

The night conjured the image of Kit as he'd stood there comforting her so many nights ago, and Lindsay had to look down to see her nightgown instead of her nude body to reassure herself that the enchantment wasn't real.

Then the image of Kit moved to embrace her as he had before, and she jumped in fright. What was happening to her? Was she going mad?

Turning toward the sink, she threw her plastic glass into it, and the noise shattered the eerie apparition. She frantically reached for the light and, switching it on, sighed in relief when the practical, everyday kitchen returned.

The next day she started a new, difficult project, specifically choosing the longest and most intricate aspect of the three-part program. She only knew one way to avoid hallucinations: to work hard and drop into bed so exhausted that not even dreams could wake her.

She sat at her desk, surrounded by flowcharts, working out the initial steps of the program. It was tough going, but the beautiful June day helped and she had opened her windows for the cool breeze blowing in off the ocean.

But along with the breeze came the drift of voices from below, including Kit's. He was evidently standing outside, giving a few last-minute pointers to a customer. It was like hearing a well-remembered and well-loved piece of music, and Lindsay often found herself sitting back with closed eyes as a connoisseur might do when listening to a favorite concerto.

She heard Kit tell Roger to watch the store, and then his voice faded into the distance. She strained to hear him return. When she stood to go to the window her flowcharts slid off her lap and floated to the floor in every direction.

"Oh, damn!" How could she have let herself get so carried away? Sitting down in frustration, she rubbed her face agitatedly. Was this how Logan had felt? Maybe she was going mad. After last night and now —she was acting practically obsessed with the man!

Kneeling on the floor to gather the scattered flowcharts, she made herself calm down. She controlled her breathing with a steady rhythm and pushed away the panic nibbling at the edges of her sanity.

"Okay, kid," she told herself. "Now you can get through this. Just take it slow, step by step." She plopped the gathered flowcharts onto her desk and sat back in her chair, resting with her feet up.

"You're going to have to face it, Lin," she finally said. "Living through this is going to be the hardest thing you've ever had to do."

The fresh, clear memories of Kit and her together tormented her. Leaning back, she closed her eyes to shut out the pain but remembered the lunches they'd laughed over, the weekends she'd spent content at his side, the dinners and long, long conversations they'd shared, and the nights she'd spent in his arms. Surely there was a way . . .

She shook her head and blinked away the tears. "You'd have more luck believing in Santa Claus," she muttered aloud.

"Ho, ho, ho," Kit's voice said from the doorway. She snatched her feet off the desk and spun around. She simply *had* to get a bell for that door!

"Kit! I didn't hear you come up the stairs."

"Saint Nicholas, if you please," he said with a grin. "I've even brought my sack." He held up a bulging white bag from the local deli. Walking over to her, he set the bag down and bent swiftly to give her a kiss.

"And I don't have to ask if you've been good, because I know you're very, very good," he murmured, his lips tasting hers again.

When he broke away he opened the sack and handed her a tightly wrapped sandwich. "I have it on good authority that you haven't been out of here all morning. Here's an avocado and jack cheese sandwich to help get you through."

She *was* hungry, and refusing it would accomplish nothing. "Thanks," she said, unwrapping it. "Who's your authority? Roger?"

"Of course. Who else has eyes on four sides of his head?" He stopped to take an enormous bite out of his sandwich. "Good kid, though. He's going to watch the shop while I give you your first Stump-jumper lesson."

"Kit, about that race . . ."

"I sent in your application this morning," he said firmly, his tone telling her he wasn't about to let her back out.

"Oh. Uh, thanks."

When they'd finished their lunch, he stood and held out his hand to her. "C'mon, honey, class is now in session."

"I really should get back to work on this program.

146

It's already giving me problems and I just started writing it."

"It's nothing compared to the problems you'll have riding an unfamiliar bike down a rocky hillside."

"Are you sure this is necessary?"

"Would you write a program for a computer you didn't know anything about?"

"Lead on, professor."

She followed him out to the parking lot, where he'd set up bright orange traffic cones around a short course. A minute later Roger wheeled the smaller Stumpjumper out to them and then, after a quick grin of encouragement to Lindsay, disappeared back into the shop.

Kit checked the brakes to make sure all the bolts were tight and then had her straddle the bike without sitting on the seat.

"Why is it a men's model? Didn't they have a women's style?" she asked, putting her leg over the cross bar. There was only an inch of clearance, but she heard Kit say "Perfect" under his breath.

"These kinds of bikes have to be as strong as they can make them," he said absently while she hopped onto the saddle and he set about checking how her feet fit into the toe straps on the pedals. "The so-called men's style with that cross tube is a much stronger design. It's the style most serious cyclists ride—male or female."

He evidently wasn't completely satisfied with the pedals, and he did something mysterious before having her straighten her leg again. "There. How's that feel?"

She had worn shorts to work that day, and she was having trouble dealing with the warm touch of his

147

hand guiding her leg movements. This kind of contact was certainly *not* the way to go about breaking off a relationship! What had she been thinking of when she'd agreed to this?

"It feels fine," she answered truthfully, though her words had little to do with how the pedals felt. As he stood, he steadied her with a firm hand at the small of her back and she trembled slightly, though the movement of the bike masked it.

"Everything looks okay. Here're the brakes," he said, pointing to the two levers in front of the handgrips. "And here're the shift levers. Leave them where they are for now—I'll show you how to work them in a minute."

The lesson lasted for another hour, and she learned not only how to use the shift levers but also when to stand up and pedal for the most results, and she picked up pointers on how to ride through mud.

That last information made her want to quit right then, but there was something about Kit's attitude that kept her quiet. He'd seemed genuinely pleased with each minuscule success, and she felt she'd be betraying him if she pulled out of the race now.

So she did the only thing she could do and went back to working on her program, finding it even harder going than before.

When the day of the race dawned, his encouragement was forgotten. Lindsay had hit a monumental snag in her program and she tried desperately to think of an acceptable excuse to back out, but she hadn't thought of anything by the time Kit arrived at her condo.

"Ready to go?" he asked, looking over her riding outfit critically. He nodded and smiled, evidently approving her narrow-legged jeans and heavy flannel shirt over the T-shirt he'd laughingly given her advertising his bike shop. He wore the one she'd given him advertising Trent Computer Systems.

"Kit, I've run into a glitch in my program and I've been working for two days trying to get past it," she said. "I think I'd better—"

"Take a break from all that mental activity," he finished for her. "The exercise will do you some good —get the blood flowing back into those sluggish brain cells."

She laughed ruefully and said, "All right."

"Good." He held out a computer printout to her. "I wanted to show you this. I've been using that program you set up to calculate proper gearing ratios. Using that computer could really be the winning edge for San Diego cyclists. It's fantastic, honey! Thanks."

His expression made her forget her excuse. A stronger person might still have tried to get out of going, but then a stronger person would've learned to defend herself against that smile.

"Your computer's come a long way—from abomination to fantastic," she said with another laugh.

It took her a minute to realize just how pleased she was at his acceptance of the computer. And if *he* could adapt to her world, the least she could do was try to adapt to his. Maybe this race would be that one last chance their relationship needed.

"I'm all packed," she said, gesturing to the small suitcase by the door. It had only been the night before that she'd found out they'd be staying in a motel near Cuyamaca State Park, but after all her procrastinating there hadn't been any use in protesting.

149

The drive to Cuyamaca took over an hour, but Kit kept Lindsay laughing or discussing computers, and she was genuinely surprised when the van pulled into the motel parking lot. They quickly checked in, then drove the last mile to the site of the race.

Cuyamaca was set in the rough foothills of the mountains, and Lindsay was both surprised at the crowd of people and amazed at the variety of bicycles that had gathered there. Several people greeted Kit, and Lindsay caught a few envious glances aimed her way, but the real envy wasn't apparent until Kit unloaded the Stumpjumpers.

After registering he carefully pinned her number on her shoulder, and she did the same for him. She smiled at the small, comfortingly domestic action and began to bend over the map he was showing her when she stopped. The solution to her programming glitch hovered right on the edge of her consciousness.

"Lindsay, are you all—" Kit began, but she waved him silent.

There, she had it! Beautiful! Of course that was the solution. She looked around her as if suddenly coming out of a fog. Bicycles? She shook her head. The answer was perfect and she had to get her hands on a computer—any computer—right away.

"Lindsay?" Kit asked, obviously concerned.

"I'm okay," she said hastily, her eyes frantically scanning the crowd and open countryside around her. "Look, I need to—" she began then stopped. What was the use? There wasn't a computer terminal within twenty-five miles of this place.

"Honey, if you're sure you're okay, we'd better get in position," he said, indicating the crowd of bicyclists gathering near a wide white banner proclaiming the CUYAMACA CLASSIC. He handed her the map and added, "Here, you'd better study the map again, too, just to make sure you understand the route."

Upset at having a solution and no way to act upon it, she took the map with ill grace. Snapping it flat, she glanced at the route and started to hand it back to Kit when her mind finally registered what she'd read. She pulled it back and read it more closely.

Water trap? Mud hole? *Rocky ravine?* She'd known the course would be up and down hills, but this was ridiculous. It looked like the route had purposely been laid out through the most unpleasant terrain possible.

She asked Kit about it and he laughed, saying, "Of course they did!" He started walking toward the starting line. When she didn't follow, he turned and called to her. "We have to hurry or we'll miss the gun."

Silently she accompanied him to the growing crowd at the starting line and mounted her bike. Looking at the excited people around her, she shook her head, thinking with disgust that if she asked them for a keyboard she'd probably get a piano. She didn't belong here! How could she have thought *this* could be a second chance for their relationship?

She leaned over to tell Kit she couldn't go through with the race, but the sharp crack of the pistol sounded before she could say anything.

The race had begun.

CHAPTER NINE

Hemmed in by the mass of bodies and bikes, Lindsay moved forward from the sheer pressure of the crowd. Her bike wobbled until her childhood instincts took over without conscious effort. The noise was raucous, and she wanted to panic, but the danger outweighed her frazzled nerves and she pedaled hard, focusing her concentration on the narrow strip of uneven downward slope in front of her.

All her mind could think of was survival and the sun-dried shoots of wild grasses surrendering to the wide, rugged tires of the Stumpjumper. Somewhere ahead of her was Kit; she didn't know how far and she didn't have time to consider it. She had to get out of the beginning pack safely and her legs pumped hard, up, down, up, down to do it.

At the bottom of the hill the route took a devious turn up through a rocky ravine. She stood to conquer it, but a voice alongside her interrupted.

"Lindsay, slow down!" Though the noise had lessened the farther from the observing crowd she had ridden, Kit still had to shout for her to hear him. "You'll hit the wall before the race is half over at that pace."

"Hit the wall?" she said, close to wailing in frustration, but she kept pedaling. "You mean there's a wall I have to ride over?" Mud holes, ravines and now a wall?

He had maneuvered around two other cyclists to ride beside her. A quick smile was all the demanding route would allow him. "No, honey. 'Hitting the wall' means your body just stops. Extreme energy depletion. All you can do is breathe."

"Okay, you win," she said, sitting on the bike saddle but still pedaling as fiercely as she could. "All I want to do is get this thing over with." She risked a glance back at the starting line and was surprised to see how far she'd already traveled. The route ahead couldn't possibly be worse than trying to ride back up that mountain.

"Finish line is straight ahead," he said, his words coming out in controlled puffs. His athlete's body had taken over, regulating his breathing to match his exertion. They rounded the top of the ravine and headed down the zigzag course, dodging boulders, clumps of unfriendly-looking bushes and the small international orange flags that marked the route.

"Straight, huh?"

He flashed her another grin. "Figuratively speaking."

"I still can't believe you got me into this," she began, but another rider came up from behind them and rudely plowed between Lindsay and Kit.

"Sorry, lover boy," the man said sarcastically, "but we're not out here for Saturday afternoon tea."

A heavy snap on his bright red jacket blew out from his side as he passed and hit Lindsay's hand gripping the handlebar. Without thinking she let go and pulled her hand back. Her bike started wobbling precariously with the sudden lack of control, and ignoring her stinging knuckles, she grabbed the handlebar to fight to remain upright. This was supposed to be fun?

"Sit loose, Lin," Kit cried. "Sink your weight!"

"For God's sake, Kit, say something useful!" she said through jaws stiff with concentration. Uneven ground snagged at the wide tires, the hard clumps of grass and rocks and prickly bushes all threatening to topple her at any minute.

"Try to relax," he said. "You can't react quick enough when your muscles are bunched with tension."

"Okay, *that* I understand," she said, consciously willing the steel knots along her shoulder to disappear.

"That's it," he said. "You're almost steady now."

She regained control of the bike, but some of the tension stayed with her. In her mind this race was a symbol of her ability to adapt to Kit's life-style, but the symbol had become tarnished and bedraggled. Broken plant stalks lay across her path, as crushed by the race as her hopes.

Pedaling with silent determination, Lindsay reached the bottom of the hill and started up the next one. She stood to give each pedal stroke more power. Was this her future? Was Kit her future?

The incline steepened and she pumped harder, trying to keep the answer away by sheer force of will. It didn't work. She looked at Kit riding easily beside her and frowned. How could she tell him their race had been called?

As they rounded the crest of the hill, Kit smiled

his heart-stopping smile. "We're doing great considering we've never done this before," he said, then ruined his humble intent by giving her a word of expert advice. "This is a steep grade, so ride your brakes—don't coast."

Between her eyes, the lines of her frown deepened. It galled her that she had to ruthlessly suppress the needlelike darts of heat she felt at his smile, but that was nothing to the rage churning inside her as she realized he was holding back for her sake.

Burrs and foxtails dug into her ankles through her socks, providing actual physical prods to her misery and anger. She opened her mouth to challenge his patronizing action, but as they rounded a turn side by side they immediately had to swerve to avoid hitting the rude man in the red jacket who had evidently taken the corner too fast and skidded out.

"Hey, watch it!" he cried, as if they were at fault for not being able to see around turns in the route.

Lindsay and Kit ignored him and rode on. A few yards past him Kit shook his head and muttered, "Squirrelly, completely squirrelly."

But she didn't hear him. Her eyes had caught the shimmer of the sun's rays on water, and it suddenly hit her that they'd arrived at the water hole.

"Kit! Do we really have to ride through that?" she said, her voice hovering on the edge of panic. A cyclist was squirming and twisting his way through it as she spoke, his tire tracks adding one more rut in the mire when he finally struggled free of the obstacle. "I thought you said this was a race, not Marine boot camp!"

"Don't let it scare you," Kit said calmly. "Keep your speed up and go into it fast and don't stop."

Seeing the expression on her face, he added, "And don't close your eyes!"

"Right!" she said, closing her eyes and holding her breath as she splashed into the shallow pool of water that was fast becoming a mud hole.

"Lindsay, keep pedaling," she heard him say, but her bike kept slowing down, the mud at the bottom of the pool grabbing the knobbly tires with a viselike grip. "Open your eyes. Lindsay!"

She came to a complete standstill and then, in slow motion, she tilted sideways and the bike—with her still on it—fell into the water.

Gasping and sputtering, she stood and faced Kit. He'd made it safely to the other side, but he'd gotten off his bike and was heading back to help her.

"Don't come near me," she said, glaring at him through the drizzle of water streaming down her face. "This is *not* my idea of a fun—puh!—time," she began, but had to stop to spit out some of the muddy water.

She could see the corners of his mouth trembling as he tried desperately to control his laughter. His eyes were amused when they traveled over her, but they also held a hint of hunger. In her anger she hadn't noticed that her flannel shirt had been pulled off her shoulders by the weight of the water, exposing the wet, nearly transparent T-shirt.

The flannel shirt felt glued in place when she tried to shrug it back on. His delighted gaze watched her movements, but then something behind her caught his eye and he swiftly closed the gap between them and hugged her tightly.

"Whaaaa?" she said, her mouth jammed into his shoulder, but her question was answered when a streak of red flashed by and an offensive laugh reached her ears.

The rude man, whom she'd secretly labeled The Creep, leered. "Couldn't wait, huh?" Fortunately he quickly rode on.

"Sorry, honey," Kit said when the man had gone, "but I didn't think you'd want him to see you like that." He gently smoothed damp tendrils of hair from her forehead and kissed her there.

"Thanks," she whispered, letting him untangle the folds of her flannel shirt and put it to rights. It wasn't fair to make her suffer his gentleness and kind humor like this. They were on opposite sides of a lonely, uncrossable chasm, and no matter how much she loved him, it could never be bridged.

He wiped off the bicycle seat and made it ridable again. "Ready to go?"

"Ready," she answered. Seeing the concern at the back of his eyes, she smiled her assurance though she sighed inwardly. It was a long, long way to the finish line.

The heat from her exertion kept her from getting a chill, and her clothes dried quickly. She was getting used to the bumpy ride, though her backbone threatened to collapse like an accordion from all the jarring, and the race suddenly seemed easier. At least that was what she kept telling herself.

But the overcast day hid the sun, and by the time they were two-thirds of the way through the race, she'd lost her sense of direction. She was completely dependent on the small orange flags and the man riding beside her to get her safely to the finish line.

They crested the top of yet another hill, and in the

distance she could see the bright white banner of the finish line. It would be smooth sailing to the end.

"Almost there, honey," Kit said encouragingly. "You're doing great!"

Great? She remembered the water hole and the gravelly wash where she'd finally had to get off the bike and walk to the top. Great as compared to what? A one-armed orangutan?

"Thanks," she said, realizing that the race had burned out much of her anger, leaving only weariness.

Going downhill, she rode the brakes as Kit had instructed, but she still kept picking up speed. He'd told her packed dirt could be even smoother to ride on than pavement, though she hadn't believed him—till now. She sped over the top of a small hillock and hit the brakes in a panic.

She'd forgotten about the mud hole! Several other riders had evidently forgotten it, too, and had been mired in the enormous patch of brown ooze. But she had no time to react before she found herself barreling on through it.

It was like trying to ride through a pool of rubber cement, and her bike inevitably became stuck. She tried to prevent a replay of the water hole, so when the bicycle started to tilt, she jumped off and managed to land on her knees instead of being completely submersed.

Slowly standing back up, she heard a shout of laughter from Kit, followed by a splurt of mud that told her he'd gotten stuck, too. Her mouth answered his grin, but her amusement went no further than that. She pulled her bike upright and walked to the edge of the mud hole. With each step she could feel the gooey stuff creeping in through the gaping seams of her old running shoes to lodge under her toes.

Fatigue combined with her agitation had hardened into a lump of frustration at the base of her skull, a lump that threatened to shatter and hurl the knife-edged shards of her anger at whatever was near.

At that moment she heard a snicker from behind her, and she whirled to see patches of a red jacket through a coating of mud.

His eyes darted from her to Kit and back again. "What, no clinch?" The Creep said, his gibing voice heavy with derision.

The mud was as slippery as roller skates, but she walked through it easily. He hadn't had the benefit of a Sunday spent skating and was having trouble staying on his feet. As with most bullies, he hadn't expected her to attack, and he watched her approach with obvious wariness. She would have laughed at his ludicrous expression if the tight hard ball of anger at the top of her backbone hadn't been throbbing and urging her onward.

She glared at him silently, then reached out with one hand and steadily pressed against his chest until, despite his frantic efforts to keep himself from falling, his feet slipped out from under him. He landed in the mud with a satisfyingly slurpy thump.

He opened his mouth, but she interrupted whatever he had been about to say. "One more word and you'll be *wearing* your derailleur." He closed his mouth so fast she heard his teeth click.

She remounted her bike and rode out of the depression that held the mud hole. Kit obviously wanted to make a comment, but her expression stopped him. Now that she'd lost control once, there was no way to keep the haze of anger away, and she pedaled the remaining distance to the finish line in determined silence.

"Hey, Kit," someone called as she and Kit were walking their bikes to the van. "We need you over here a sec."

Mutely she watched him open the back of the vehicle and in her stupor vaguely wondered how he had any strength left at all. As soon as she'd stepped off the bicycle after crossing the finish line, her body had rebelled at the treatment she'd given it.

Now, tired and weak from the long ride, Lindsay couldn't keep her own muscles from trembling; any minute she could lose the slight control she did have and collapse.

She barely caught Kit's murmured "I'll be right back" before he went over to the group that had hailed him. For a long moment she just stood at the back of the van until her head fell forward as she almost fell asleep. Snapping her head back up, she made herself walk to the passenger door, ignoring the drying clumps of mud falling off her jeans.

She looked inside the open door of the van at the high passenger seat. That step hadn't looked half so steep this morning. Just as she braced herself for the big climb, a hand on her elbow propelled her and her shrieking muscles up into the seat.

"Honey, a couple of riders haven't come back yet," Kit said. "They're probably only stragglers and'll show up in the next few minutes, but if they don't we'll have to go out and look for them." He squeezed her hand. "You look beat. Listen, I'll drop you off at the motel and then come back here. They should have arrived by then if they're going to."

She was sorry others might be lost, but it was

difficult to work up proper compassion when she was feeling so lost herself right then.

"If you're sure you won't be needed right away, I'll take you up on that offer," she managed to get out. At least she could talk, though her jaw seemed to be the only place that didn't hurt.

Once alone in the motel room, she collapsed in a chair and didn't move for almost an hour. She must've ridden the last few miles of the race on sheer willpower without knowing it. Now she understood where the term "hitting the wall" came from, because that was exactly what she felt like she'd done.

Looking around the bare motel room at the bleached-white chenille bedspread and the bolted-down cheap furniture—whoever named that style Danish modern obviously had had something against the Danes—it seemed appropriate that this was where her relationship with Kit was to end. Nothing to make her sentimental and put off telling him that whatever was between them wasn't enough to overcome their differences.

It was over. It had to be. After today she knew she could never begin to keep up with him or his world. She'd been right in the beginning—he was way out of her league.

She laughed ruefully at her inadvertent pun—one of the organizations he belonged to was the League of American Wheelmen.

Fantasies should stay just that—safe, innocuous flights of fancy one could tack to a wall and walk away from. But she didn't need her imagination to tell her how Kit's arms felt around her; her memory vividly recalled it. And it wasn't the touch of a paper poster her fingers tingled to remember but the feel of his skin under her hand.

Stop it! She glanced guiltily at the door as if she expected Kit to barge in at that moment. Then she realized how long he'd been gone and frowned. Had something happened? She shook her head, thinking it was useless to speculate but knowing that didn't make the waiting any easier. Soon she'd lose her courage altogether. She closed her eyes and let her head fall back. When had she become such a coward?

After catching herself dozing off for the third time, she slowly pried her sore body out of the chair, every muscle shrieking a protest as she moved. Staggering into the shower, she let her clothes stay on the floor where they fell because she had no energy to do anything else.

The shower revived her slightly, giving her a false sense of energy. "Okay, Kit," she said aloud to the empty room. "I've tried—I've honestly tried—to make a go of our relationship, but I think we both know we're just too different. . . . No, that's too vague."

She donned her nightgown and robe and tried again. "Kit, there's no denying that there's something between us, but our life-styles are too different for us ever to be able to have anything like a long-term relationship." She made a face in the mirror and said, "Ugh. What a ridiculously convoluted way to say 'Kit, I love you but if we stayed together we'd both feel like we'd been written into a bad closed loop with no way out.' " *Just like Mara and Logan,* she added silently.

She'd spoken without thinking, and the force of her words hit her like a physical blow. Collapsing onto the bed, she covered her face with her hands. How could she have allowed herself to step right into the same trap Logan had barely escaped from! The

162

pain in her chest grew and she fell back onto the bed, hugging herself, heedless of the tears staining the pillowcase.

It hurt! Oh, how loving someone could hurt!

Emotionally and physically exhausted, she was on the verge of sleep when Kit finally came in, too far into unconsciousness to rouse her weary mind. Vaguely, as if from a great distance, she heard him whisper.

"Lindsay? Honey, are you awake?"

"Mmmm?" was all she managed.

"We spent four hours looking for those riders, only to find out they'd given up fifteen minutes into the race and gone home!" He paused for a moment and she felt him leaning over her recumbent form. "Lin? Never mind, honey, I'll tell you in the morning. Go back to sleep."

She slid back into sleep as she heard him turn on the shower, only to wake slightly when he slid into bed next to her.

Kit, I love you but . . . His arm slid around her waist and he snuggled up to her.

"Good night, Lin-love," he murmured.

Her silent tears fell unheeded.

"I hurt everywhere!" Lindsay said, climbing out of Kit's van in front of his house. That morning, after a night disturbed by a recurrence of her frightening dream, she'd realized the old dingy motel room wasn't the place to end a relationship and had held off telling him. It took her half the drive home to convince herself she hadn't just lost her courage.

"What you need is a bout in the whirlpool and

then a nice hot dinner," he said. He unlocked the door and stood back to let her in.

"Kit—" she began.

He held up a hand to stop her words. "Hot tub, dinner, and then you can yell at me for not telling you the race was going to be that hard. Okay?"

She nodded, mute with disgust at her own cowardice.

The warm roiling water did help her sore muscles, but the wonderful feast he fixed her did nothing for her fortitude. She quickly finished the plate of zucchini lasagna, which he'd covered with a variation of his fabulous marinara sauce. Carrots added a surprising touch of sweetness, and as she savored the last bite, it suddenly dawned on her that she hadn't thought of his cooking as "vegetarian" in a long time. In fact, it no longer seemed different at all.

Did that mean she was starting to overcome the differences in their life-styles? *Nonsense! Get on with it. This pussy-footing around isn't fair to either one of us.*

She sat on the sofa next to him, trying to frame her words properly. He gently teased the tiny hairs in front of her ear and smiled, but she turned toward him and his smile disappeared when he saw the troubled look in her eyes.

"Is something wrong, honey?"

"Kit—" she began, then faltered. Taking a deep breath, she started again. "Kit, do you remember that day I came down to your shop and saw the Stumpjumper? The day I decided to go on this crazy race?"

The normally brilliant lights in his green eyes were dim with concern. The low monotone of her voice had evidently cued him that something was wrong, and he nodded warily. He sat utterly still.

"At the time you asked me if I'd come down for anything specific, and I said no." She stopped and looked at her clasped hands, studying the intricate patterns of lines across her knuckles. *Say it!*

"That wasn't the truth. I *had* come down for a specific reason." She looked up into his eyes. "I'd come down to tell you our relationship wasn't working."

He said nothing but sat there in stunned silence, staring at her as if someone had suddenly cut out his heart and was holding it up for him to see. Then he slumped into the cushions and looked away from her, his eyes flitting around the room as if not trusting them to land on any object.

"How can you say that?" he whispered. "Don't you *want* it to work?"

She closed her eyes tightly to ward off the pain howling through her mind and heart. "It's not what I *want*, Kit. It's just the way things are."

"Damn it, no!" he said, finally reacting the way she'd imagined. "It's *not* 'just the way things are'! You've got to work at any relationship, Lin. Maybe ours more than most, but it was working. We've been happy together—you can't deny that. How can you throw that away?"

"We're too different," she said, pleading with him to understand. "I'm a computer freak who punches in code all day. You're geared to physical things, while the only exercise I ever get is mathematical. I don't fit into your world."

"You fit perfectly!"

She leaned back into the sofa's cushions and closed her eyes with a sigh. She had expected anger from him, not obstinance. "Our life-styles are incompatible on the most basic levels."

"We can work it out."

"I don't think we can," she said, bolstered by an unwelcome image from her disturbing dream.

"No, I don't accept that," he stated flatly, though his face looked unexpectedly wild and frightened.

He still sat close to her, but his touch had been withdrawn. How she missed his gentle, idle caresses already! Jumping up, she ran to her purse and pulled out a bundle of small pieces of paper.

"Will you accept this then?" She threw the papers at him and watched them flutter onto his lap and the sofa. On the ride home she'd managed to remember part of the solution to her programming glitch and had wanted to write it down before she lost it altogether. There was no note pad to write on, so she'd desperately torn out the deposit slips from the back of her checkbook and wrote the lines of code all over those.

"I almost went crazy yesterday," she said. "Just before the race the solution to my problem hit me, and what could I do about it? Nothing! I should have been back at my office sitting at the keyboard, but what was I doing instead? Riding down a mountain on a bicycle!"

"I still don't see the problem," he said stubbornly. But the tone of his voice told her he did.

"I think you do," she said softly. "You go to races, or if not races, then training rides. You even ride to work. Riding *is* your work. And where am I all this time? *Away* from my work.

"Just as cycling is your life, the world of computers is mine. And those worlds are too far apart."

"No!" Being the physical man he was, he stood

and gripped her arms, oblivious to the bits of paper falling to the carpet. "Of course we're different! We're as different as a man and woman *should* be!" His hands slid up her shoulders and gently cupped her face. "And there were times when you didn't seem to mind those differences," he said softly, his thumbs rubbing the small protrusion of flesh in front of her ears.

The rustling from his touch was loud in her ears and in her heart. How easy it would be to throw herself into his arms at that moment. His words would have been specious in anyone less powerfully male, and she would have been a fool if she didn't acknowledge the strength of the sexual bond between them—even now her blood was heating from his touch.

She forced herself to pull away from him. "Don't twist my words, Kit. That look in your eyes tells me you know it's not lust, not 'me Tarzan, you Jane,' between us."

"It's certainly not platonic," he said roughly, his hands clenching. He stood only a few feet away, but Lindsay could feel the pain and frustration radiating from him. He looked so hurt.

"A man and a woman make love to express an emotional bond that can't be put into words," he said, running his hand through his hair. He looked at her intently for a long moment, then stepped to within inches of her but did not touch her.

She was supremely conscious of his breath on her face and the rhythm of his breathing, almost as if that vital life force were a part of her own body's function, while the desperation in his eyes bore into her, filling her with all the pain and hurt and wrenching agony that love could heap into a heart.

"Kit . . ." she began, hoping to forestall him, hoping to make him see she'd wanted to avoid pain, not cause it.

He didn't let her finish. "An emotional bond you're denying by saying our relationship won't work because of vague differences. But if we didn't have that bond, then we never had anything but lust."

His hand came up and stopped a hair's breadth from her cheek. In a ragged whisper he said, "You are everything that has ever excited me, and enticed me, and enthralled me about women. Was that only lust, Lindsay? Was there nothing more than raw animal passion in your smiles, in your laughter, in my dreams?"

His hand dropped to his side as if suddenly lifeless, and he walked away. Keeping his face from her, he half leaned, half sat on the back of the sofa and stared into the kitchen with sightless eyes.

"Perhaps it was," he said sadly. Suddenly his chin dropped to his chest, as if his neck could no longer support the weight of his sadness.

"Kit," she said softly. "It wasn't—I never meant to hurt you like this." But she knew her words were as trite as they sounded. She had been a selfish fool, blinded so by her own fear of feeling pain that she had inflicted far worse on someone she loved. "I was afraid it would be like Mara. . . ."

"No, Lindsay," he said harshly. "Mara's just a bogeyman you use to frighten children." He turned, letting his eyes meet hers, and Lindsay flinched at the naked pain and longing she saw there.

Kit looked away again. "Please go. There's something wrong about seeing a grown man cry."

Lindsay let her eyes travel over his broad back,

bowed with emotion, and repressed a desperate need to run and embrace him. How could she have hurt him so?

She took a step toward his slumped frame. With a shudder of self-hate and revulsion at herself for what she'd done, she stopped. Did she want to see how much more harm she could inflict on the man she loved?

Quietly walking toward the door, she turned and looked at the anguished man one last time. "Goodbye, Christopher Nathaniel Hawthorne," she whispered, too low for him to hear. "I love you."

The door closed behind her with a tiny click, and she walked into the darkness of the night and of her life.

CHAPTER TEN

Lindsay stared unseeing at the computer terminal screen, the small green letters forming a pale backdrop to the images in her mind. It was a warm Saturday in mid-August, and she could hear voices from the bike shop below drifting up through the open window.

The week after the race had proved more difficult than she could have imagined. Without having to be told, Roger had immediately seen that something was wrong between Lindsay and Kit and had bounded up the stairs to her office when his employer had refused to answer his questions. Why, he'd wondered, had Kit stopped talking about retiring, stopped talking about having Lindsay at his side when he announced it at the race, stopped talking about much of anything?

It wasn't until after she'd finally managed to send the young man away, his questions unanswered, that she'd begun staring at the computer screen, her eyes not shedding the tears her heart weeped. She hadn't known Kit had wanted her at his side when he announced his retirement at the race, and now she couldn't make herself think of what it might have meant. So she sat. And for a long while it seemed as if something vital within her had been severed.

Though she would go through a program by rote, her life, her *real* life in her mind was made up of memories: memories of joy in sunshine and laughter in a mist-shrouded morning. And images of remembered love and passion. But the memories of their lovemaking were the most potent, and her whole body ached with the loss.

A crash from outside brought her to the present. She ran to the window and saw Kit slowly, stiffly standing up beside a mangled bicycle on the curb. With screeching tires, a small brown sports car darted into traffic, and in a second she realized the careless driver must not have seen Kit as he'd pulled into the parking lot and had tried to pull in at the same time.

It wasn't until she exhaled in a rush when Kit waved away Rog's assistance that she knew she'd been holding it, fearing for his safety. She had to get back to work on her program, but she let her eyes follow Kit as he walked up the sidewalk to his shop. He never looked up.

"I tell you, he's gonna kill himself," Roger said, blithely sitting on the edge of her desk and swinging one leg. "After that accident a couple of weeks ago, you could see he was hurtin'—no bones broken, just bruises and all—but he just kept on ridin'.

"Nobody trains *that* hard, I don't care how old he is. I mean, like, he's up before dawn, ridin' all the way to Del Mar and back—*Del Mar!*—*every* morning."

"It's only two weeks before the race," Lindsay

171

countered. "Surely his training would intensify then." She was tired and weary and didn't know how long she could take Rog's unfailing cheerfulness. Even when he was concerned about Kit, there was something irrepressible about him.

She didn't need Rog to tell her Kit had been training too hard. Without making any conscious decision to do so, she'd been coming to her office early in the morning, and from the obscurity of her window, she had watched him ride up the street each day. He'd started to look gaunt, and she had hoped it was just his harsh training regimen that had made him so, but Rog's words precluded that.

"Intensify, sure, but he's been doing this *all* summer. I tell you, I'm worried about him. At the rate he's going he'll be lucky to survive *until* the race, let alone ride in it." His leg stopped swinging for a moment and he peered closely at her as she sat back in her chair, staring out the window.

"And speakin' of survivin'," Roger added, "I'd say you're not doin' too hot yourself." He shook his head and stood up with a jump. "Ya know, a friend of mine told me he was madly in love with this girl. I told him if he'd get a look at you two, he wouldn't be so free with his emotions."

Fortunately her brother walked in at that moment and she wasn't forced to hear more of Roger's advice to the lovelorn. But her relief quickly changed to pique when Logan's eyes narrowed at seeing the dark circles under her own eyes.

When Roger said his good-byes and sauntered out, her brother only nodded vaguely in his direction. "I knew it. You've been driving yourself like a maniac, Lin. Do you realize you've spent the entire summer indoors?"

172

"Loge, quit fussing. I'm fine," she said peevishly.

"No, you're not. Now close this place up," he told her. He wrinkled his nose at the pile of fast-food wrappers in her overflowing trash can. "I'm taking you out to get a decent meal and then I'm taking you home for a long summer's nap. Any objections? Good."

Without realizing it Logan took her to the same coffee shop where she and Kit had accompanied him so long ago, and it was a further piece of bad luck that the waiter seated them in the same corner booth they'd had before. Lindsay could almost feel her back pressing into Kit's side.

A carafe of wine was delivered after their order had been taken. Her brother silently poured the deep red burgundy into their glasses while watching her trying to suppress a yawn.

"Okay, sis," he said, setting the carafe down with a firm thud. "I know you're tired, but I want to know what is going on between you and Kit."

She swirled the wine and watched the rivulets etch their way back down the inside of the round glass bowl. "What's going on between me and Kit? Nothing. Zip. Zero. Null and void."

"Why? What happened?"

She shrugged as nonchalantly as she could, not knowing how much of her inner anguish was revealed on her face. "I told him I didn't think things were working between us. Oh, Logan, we're so different. I was afraid of what might happen."

With the lightning understanding of a twin, Logan said, "Afraid he might pull a Mara on you?" She nodded.

"Oh, Lin, Mara and I rarely laughed together, or even talked," he told her, a sad note creeping into his

173

voice. "But you were always smiling with Kit. You were *happy*. And to be honest, when I saw that you were so happy, I forgot about all my dire warnings.

"I thought you'd forgotten about them, too. I only voiced them in the first place because I didn't want you hurt the way Mara had hurt me. But I soon saw it was completely different with you two."

He lowered his eyes, and she could tell he was uneasy. "Why don't you go back and tell him you'd like to try making it work, Lin. You were happy when you were with him and now you're unhappy without him. That tells me everything I need to know."

"Logan, you don't understand! We have nothing in common! That last race was horrible," she said, her voice falling to a whisper. "I thought if I could handle that, maybe it could work between us. But it was a disaster from beginning to end."

"It didn't sound like it was too great for Kit either," Logan said. "Maybe you picked the wrong testing ground."

"No, it wasn't just the race itself. I was *dying* to get my hands on a computer—*any* computer—to try out a routine I'd just thought of, but there wasn't one within twenty-five miles of that place."

"So take one along. There are plenty of reliable battery-operated portables on the market. The whole idea behind the move to a separate office was to free you from all the nuts-and-bolts stuff—we've got an entire software department to do that, Lin." He reached out and gave her hand an affectionate squeeze. "You're one of the best in the industry when it comes to thinking up innovative software packages, and you don't have to use Trent computers to do that."

Lindsay just stared at him. A portable computer! It was a beautiful solution—a summer too late.

Logan eyed his sister shrewdly. "You're thinking it's too late for you and Kit, aren't you?"

"It is, Loge. I hurt him terribly."

Apparently off the subject, he said, "You remember that big blowout we had when you'd just met Kit? Well, the next day I got drunk—not stinking drunk, just high enough so when Sue asked me what was wrong, I told her. And you know what she said?"

She shook her head, still reeling from the effects of his earlier comment. The answer to her dilemma had been staring at her from the cover of countless computer magazines and she'd never seen it! Lindsay Trent was damn well going to start keeping her eyes open. And her ears, catching the last of what Logan had said.

He paused to make sure she was listening, then continued. "She told me it's not only your love but *being* loved that makes a relationship worthwhile. With Mara it wasn't just that she'd betrayed my love but that she'd withdrawn hers—I had a double whammy to get over."

"And are you over it?" she asked cautiously.

He shrugged, an unconscious imitation of her earlier unsuccessful attempt at nonchalance. "Yeah. Mostly. I don't miss her, or pine for her as I did, but there'll always be a part of my heart sealed off." He shrugged again. "But I've known love, and I think I'm better for it. And Kit had your love—at least for a while. That's a precious gift to give anyone, Lin."

She was quiet on the ride home, answering her brother's questions with low monosyllables. Logan had used the past tense in describing her love for Kit, but Lindsay knew that her love was as strong as ever, a love not only in the present tense but the future as well. Was there such a thing as a forever tense?

The remaining time before the race passed quickly. She was careful not to let Logan's words affect her, pushing them away to the far corners of her mind whenever a tiny, fragile shoot of hope would blossom. But though she was able to control her conscious mind, those small stalks of hope took root in her subconscious to flower in her dreams. She didn't discover the strength of those dreams until a few days before the race.

An early Santa Ana had hit, leaving San Diego dry and hot, and she was forced to open every window and door in her office to survive. Temperature records were being set every day, and she spent the nights covered with a damp towel because the power demand hadn't allowed her to run an air conditioner.

It was Tuesday, and the race was set to begin in Sacramento on the following Saturday. She'd long since given up working in the heat and had rolled her chair over to an open window. Leaning back in her chair, the only part of her limp body that moved was her right hand while she slowly fanned herself. At first, half-dozing as she was, she didn't hear the voices from the street rising to her window like shimmering waves of heat from the hot pavement.

"Look, Roger," she vaguely heard Kit's voice say, "you're paid to watch the counter, okay? Now get me a couple extra pairs of sew-ups." The muffled clangs of metal against metal told her he must be packing the van for the race. He sounded different to her, though, as might an actor who had changed roles.

"How can you worry about tires when you should be worryin' about stayin' alive," Rog said, his words heavy with exasperation. "Ever since you and Lin broke up, you've been—"

Kit's angry words interrupted him. "Roger, get this straight. *She* broke it off, okay? None of this *we* stuff." The door to the van slammed shut. "Sorry, Rog, I shouldn't have snapped at you like that. The heat's getting to me, I guess. But the past is past. We can't ever bring it back—no matter how much we want to."

Lindsay's fan had long since stopped its desultory fluttering. Her eyes stared sightlessly off into the distance, as they had so often the past few months, but the dullness had been replaced with the glittering tinsel of speculation. ". . . no matter how much we want to."

Their voices broke in on her musings. "I'll be staying at the Red Lion Inn," Kit said, apparently to Roger. "And don't worry—I can get someone up there to run the feeding station for me." The van started up then, and she couldn't make out the rest of Rog's words.

The idea came to her that night, but it took her until Thursday to work up the courage to talk to Roger. She was beginning to realize that that young man saw a great deal more than he let on, and that behind his casual surfer pose was a kind heart and bright mind.

"Rog," Lindsay began, leaning on the bike shop's counter, "how long did you say Kit would be up in Sacramento?" She played with the toe clips in the display that sat on the glass top.

His eyes narrowed in a knowing expression that

sat oddly on his eighteen-year-old face. "I didn't," he said, grinning at her.

"Rog . . ."

His grin widened. "He'll probably drive back on Monday or Tuesday, depending on how tired he is." He innocently began straightening the colorful display of water bottles. "A lot of the cyclists are staying at the Red Lion Inn—some package deal with the race sponsor. I hear it's a real nice place. A lot of people stay there during their vacations in the state capital."

"Do they?"

"Yeah."

Their eyes met in perfect understanding, and Lindsay burst out laughing. It felt good to laugh again; and where there was laughter, there was hope.

The plane didn't arrive in Sacramento until late Friday evening, and by the time the taxi eventually pulled up in front of the large inn complex, Lindsay could do little but crawl into bed exhausted. She'd been running on nervous energy alone for days, but now everything depended on her getting up at dawn the following day.

The next morning she showered and purposely left her hair unbraided. She dressed carefully in a pair of form-fitting white jeans, a silk blouse in a blue that matched her eyes and that she left unbuttoned down to *there,* and a pair of ankle-high boots. Her lips curved into a smile when she examined herself in the mirror. She looked casual, comfortable and sensational.

As she put the finishing touches on her makeup, she had the absurd feeling of being a soldier arming himself for battle. But it was a battle—and she was fighting for her life.

The starting line was crowded, as she'd expected, but when her eyes found him as he was putting on his helmet, suddenly there were no crowds, no chattering conversations, only one tall, slender, golden-haired man. He was intent on the race and hadn't seen her in the packed sidelines, and as she watched the smooth flow of his muscles under the shiny black skin suit, the too-long-banked embers began to flame.

She walked toward him through the crowd, her eyes constantly following the controlled grace of his movements as he bent to speak to an official and then made minor adjustments to his bicycle. It wasn't until he was rising from checking the snug fit of his water bottle that his green gaze fell on her.

She stood only a few feet away, and the silence between them was louder than the roar of the spectators. There was a tense air about him that couldn't fully be explained by prerace concentration, and the tightness around his eyes hadn't been there in the early part of summer. *Why didn't he say anything?*

Straightening her shoulders, she swallowed what pride she had left. "Good luck with the race," she said in as calm a voice as she could manage. "I saw a map of the route earlier this morning. It looks pretty rough. But Rog said you'd been training up in Del Mar, so I don't think you'll have any trouble."

He eyed her narrowly but said nothing. After a long minute he nodded his thanks, as he would to any casual well-wisher, and returned to his preparations.

Stunned at his rebuff, Lindsay forced herself to smile and walk back to the sidelines, never noticing

179

that Kit watched her retreating back until she was lost among the crowd.

"Lindsay! Am I glad to see you!" a woman's voice shouted above the tumult. Lindsay turned around and saw a hand waving in her direction, a hand that quickly appeared with Jenny on the other end of it.

"Thank goodness you two have made up," she said, hugging Lindsay. She had obviously misread the situation, but she went right on talking before she could be set straight. "I've never seen a man drive himself so hard. He went from being deliriously happy to just plain delirious."

"Hey, welcome back," another cyclist said cheerfully. He shook her hand and then was good-naturedly pushed aside as yet another cyclist from San Diego came forward.

"I'll bet Kit was glad to see you," the woman said with a smile. "I know we are." She pulled Lindsay close and said confidentially, indicating a fourth member of the group still trying to make his way through the crowd, "Listen, do you think you could help Tom when we get back? He got this fancy electronic gadget that measures pulse and distance and has a timer on it and God knows what else, and none of us can make heads or tails of it. I know you helped Kit with his computer . . ."

They were welcoming her back! Lindsay's head was spinning with the implications. How could she have thought she couldn't be part of their world when they accepted her so readily? She'd obviously blundered and misinterpreted the situation badly, but would Kit accept her quite so easily?

The bullhorn blared at that moment, announcing the impending start of the race. Her eyes found Kit immediately in the jumble of riders hunched over

180

their bikes, and she let her gaze wander over him freely, his slender lines and tensed muscles all familiar and dear to her. She loved him desperately and wanted him in every way a woman could want a man.

Her mind told her there was no hope that he'd forgive her. But she'd let her mind rule her once before, with disastrous results. Now it was time to let her heart do the talking.

Turning, she saw Jenny watching her with a quizzical expression. The cyclist winked at Lindsay and said, "C'mon. Let's make sure we get to the feeding station on time."

Following a map the officials had given her, Jenny drove the bike shop's van to the halfway point of the long race. Kit wouldn't arrive for several hours, and after Jenny explained to Lindsay what to do when the racers showed up, they sat in the back of the van and relaxed.

But Lindsay couldn't be completely at her ease, and her eyes constantly swept the road in the distance to check for the first appearance of the cyclists. The gesture had become a habit by the time the riders did show up, and it took a second glance before she realized that the pack was indeed heading their way.

Feeding stations were normally on hills so the cyclists would naturally slow down. She cursed her boots as she grabbed the bottles and fruit Jenny held out to her and ran to the edge of the roadway. The riders hit the bottom of the hill and started to slow. Spotting Kit, she began to jog so she could run alongside him to hand him the water and such.

"Kit, here!" she shouted, dodging others doing the

same thing. He maneuvered over to her, and she squeezed a steady stream of water over his perspiring head.

"That feels good—thanks," he said, shaking his head. She opened and handed him the bottle of orange juice. His eyes kept darting to her, but he was too busy gulping down the juice to say anything more right then.

"How are you doing? Any cramping?" she asked, trying to remember what Jenny had told her to ask. It was hard running uphill in her boots, and she was starting to pant as she exchanged the empty orange juice bottle for a banana.

He shook his head. "No, not yet," he said. He devoured the first banana and she handed him another one. Glancing at the fast-approaching crest of the hill, he asked tersely, "Why are you here?"

She didn't have much time, and all her explanations would take hours. Why not tell him the simple truth and leave the explanations for later? She held out a fresh water bottle and took his old empty one.

"Because I love you, Kit," she said between gulps of air.

His eyes held an odd glint as he let his gaze wander over her disheveled elegance. The top of the hill was only a few feet away, and still he said nothing! But just as he reached the crest, his gloved hand stretched out and tucked her hair behind her ear. In a second he'd speeded up and reentered the race.

For a long time she just stood at the top of the hill and watched the riders as they faded into the distance, her fingers lightly rubbing her ear.

"Are you all right, Lindsay?" Jenny asked, walking up behind her.

A tentative smile gathered strength. "I'm fine, Jenny, just fine."

Hours later the starting line had been converted into a finish line, with officials making a last-minute check of the camera aimed along the black stripe painted across a wider white strip, ready in case of a photo finish. Lindsay stood next to Jenny and the others near the barricades that had been set up to keep the enthusiastic crowd out of the racers' path. Someone behind her kept leaning forward, jabbing his elbows into her waist as he tried to spot the riders when they appeared.

A cheer went up from the spectators farther down the road—the first of the racers had ridden into view. Suddenly elbows and crushed toes no longer mattered. She leaned forward, hoping to catch a glimpse of Kit. There were four cyclists close together leading the rest. Was Kit among them?

Then the third cyclist started moving up fast. It was Kit. At the twenty-five-meter mark he passed the second cyclist and was hard on the wheels of the leader.

The crowd started jumping and yelling, and most of the shouts of encouragement were lost in the general din. But that didn't stop Lindsay. She cheered him on at the top of her lungs, waving her hands and jumping with the rest of them.

All of a sudden a chant started growing among the crowd. "Sprint! Sprint!" Kit pulled even with the leader, and for a few meters they rode wheel to wheel. He looked exhausted, and Lindsay started to doubt if he could make the bicycle go those last few inches to pass the leader. Then an echo of a memory whispered in her ear: *My specialty's the sprint.* Her voice joined the chanting spectators.

And then he did it. At the last minute he called up a reserve of strength from she knew not where, and she watched as his every muscle stood out from the exertion as he broke away and crossed the finish line a full length ahead of the rider in second place.

Pandemonium reigned as officials ran along the sidelines, frantically trying to keep the crowd from spilling into the roadway in front of the rest of the racers. When the race had officially ended, Lindsay was carried along with the mass of bouncing, cheering bodies to the platform set up for the winners.

A bottle of champagne opened with a pop, barely discernible in the roar, and soon the top three riders were doused in the foaming stuff. On the platform Kit stood in the middle, laughing and smiling at the crowd and brushing back his hair, dripping with champagne. But his eyes were never still as he constantly scanned the mass of cheering people before him.

The medaling ceremony was brief, but as the gold medal was slid over Kit's head, Lindsay found herself crying with happiness. Cameras were snapping all around her as the race officials gave the three winners victory bouquets and then stepped back to let them receive their full glory.

Then Kit's restless gaze found her, and she could hear no sound but the beating of her heart. He jumped off the platform and burrowed his way through the congratulating crowd to her. Without a second's hesitation he caught her up in an embrace and kissed her fervently.

The crowd went wild, but she was alone with him

as his lips demanded that there be no holding back, no denial of their love.

"I love you, Lin-love," he whispered. "I love you. We can make it work."

"I know we can," she whispered back. She wanted to say more, so much more, but the people demanded their victor.

But before he was swept away by the crowd, he pressed the victory bouquet into her arms and said, "I still can't give you a blue rose, caliph's daughter, only my heart."

"A most rare and precious gift," she answered, crying and clutching the flowers tightly.

Struggling to resist the force of the crowd pulling him away from her, he bent and murmured in her ear. "I'll wait for you tonight. I'm in room seventy-five seventeen."

She only had time to nod before the pressure of the moving mass of humanity separated them.

Early that evening Lindsay showered and changed into a sapphire blue dress that hugged her curves. Walking through the inn lobby to reach Kit's room, there was a certain happy swing to her hips that drew appreciative glances.

Her steps slowed as she approached his room. This meeting would be their first in private since she'd broken off their relationship. Would he regret his impulsive behavior of that afternoon?

She squared her shoulders and reached out to rap on the door. Whatever he might say, she owed him this, she knew, and knocked. The door, however, hadn't been properly latched and her knuckles pushed it open instead of announcing her.

Kit was lying prone on a portable masseur's table,

facing away from her while a burly masseur kneaded his muscles. The man was working on the racer's shoulders and, facing the door, saw her come in. He started to react, but she motioned him to silence. Extracting a twenty-dollar bill from her clutch, she waved it and gestured for him to leave.

He grunted and said, "Jus' a sec'," to Kit and walked out the door, taking his duffel bag and the offered money with him.

A white towel covered Kit's slim hips, and she could see that he'd closed his eyes for the relaxing massage.

"George?" he asked sleepily, keeping his eyes closed. "Anything the matter?"

Setting her purse on the dresser, she went to him and slowly began to rub his back. She felt him relax at the resumption of the massage, then a moment later realize that the touch was different. He suddenly turned and gathered her into his arms.

"No, nothing's the matter," she said in a hoarse whisper. Neither of them seemed to notice that his towel had slipped to the floor.

It felt so good to be held close to him again. It felt so good to touch the hard, smooth velour of his skin again. His lips nipped a row of kisses on her neck and into her hair.

"Lin-love," he whispered, kissing her over and over with a hunger that she readily matched. "My Lin-love." He pulled her down on top of the massage table, their bodies twined.

Logan had been right. Loving and being loved were two halves of a glorious whole.

Much later her head rested on his shoulder as he caressed the curves of her naked side. "Why did you come back?" he asked softly, as if half-afraid of the answer. "I was so alone."

"Oh, Kit, I was such a fool. I only left because I was so scared of being hurt. And I ended up inflicting a pain on both of us that was far worse than anything I could have imagined. I don't see how you can forgive me."

"Honey, love's a package deal and forgiveness is part of it." He hugged her as they lay on the massage table, her clothes littering the floor around them. "I've won two races today," he said in a voice full of emotion. "But the gold medal from *this* race is going to go right here." He drew her left hand to his lips and kissed the fourth finger. "And we can toast each other with the victory cup at our wedding."

"Are you sure you want to?" Lindsay asked, her voice reflecting her body's shiver as his arm tightened around her so he could nibble on the sensitive skin behind her ear. "For a lifetime? Don't you think it'd be better if we took it a day at a time? We're still so different. . . ."

"Differences? It'll take a lifetime to discover them all," he said, his words muffled by the perfumed cascade of her hair. "Besides, don't the French have something to say about differences?"

"*Vive la . . . ?*"

"Mmmhmmm," he murmured, his lips sampling one of those exciting differences. "A lifetime, Lin-love, a lifetime."

LOOK FOR NEXT MONTH'S
CANDLELIGHT ECSTASY ROMANCES ®:

Candlelight
Ecstasy Romances™

$1.95 each

Candlelight Ecstasy Romances™

Candlelight
Ecstasy Romances™